Contents

WHICH IS A MORE SHAMEFUL CALLING,
TO BE A JUGGLER OR A THIEF?

≈ Old saying ≈

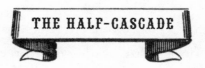

THE HALF-CASCADE

F^COR the first time in his life, Sullivan Mintz, standing in his underwear, was doing a half-cascade with *four* balls. He was trying not to become so excited that he would overthrow a ball, or look down at his hands, or make any of the million tiny moves that would throw him off.

The half-cascade is the classic pattern of juggling, the balls crossing one another as they rise up and fall again into the juggler's hands before being thrown once more. It is an elegant sight when done well, the juggler appearing to move as effortlessly as if he were raising a glass of water to his lips.

The truth is, just about anyone who works at it can learn to do a half-cascade with three balls. Kids, middle-aged men, grandmothers. But four balls—that's something else entirely, a whole new level of difficulty. It takes a leap of courage and coordination, not to mention speed. It takes far more practice—weeks, sometimes months. But done well, it looks not only elegant, but wondrous.

Sullivan had started juggling six months ago, but it was only in the last five weeks that he had attempted four balls. And until this moment, Sullivan had messed up every time. Yet he had persisted, obsessively practicing before school, after school, at bedtime, any chance he got. He took his soft juggling balls to school and practiced at lunch, in an empty classroom where nobody would see him. Even when he wasn't practicing, it felt as if he were, the balls rising and falling in his mind, his fingers opening and closing the way people sometimes moved their lips silently when they read.

Five weeks. Five weeks, every chance he got. And now he had it.

Sullivan, who was eleven years and seven months old, was once called by a teacher "the most average kid I've ever known." And it was true that his grades were average across the board, his height was average, even his hair color was somewhere between blond and brown. The remark had been made to another teacher, but Sullivan and several other students had overheard, including a beefy kid named Samuel Patinsky, who was always on the lookout for somebody to torment. From that day forward, Samuel had started calling Sullivan "Mr. Average." Sullivan despised the nickname, but he didn't see what he could do about it. His friend Norval had suggested that he call Samuel Patinsky "Mr. Below Average." But Sullivan had no desire to get punched in the face.

He had taken up juggling on the advice of Manny Morgenstern, one of the oldest residents of the Stardust Home for Old People. Manny was eighty-one. He had suggested juggling one afternoon when Sullivan was feeling pretty unhappy about just about everything. Like having only one friend at school. And being taunted by Samuel Patinsky. And having the kinds of chores that other kids didn't have. And having a mother who was known by the embarrassing title of the Bard of Beanfield. And having a little sister who everyone thought was adorable when, in fact, she was the slimiest, most scheming creature alive.

Manny might have suggested all kinds of things, such as learning guitar or taking karate lessons. He was trying to think of something that would improve

Sullivan's coordination and perhaps give him some confidence. And that wouldn't cost his parents, whose business was having what is politely called a cash flow problem, very much money. But juggling just seemed right.

"Once you start," Manny had said, "you'll want to juggle all the time. Your parents are going to have to tell you to stop. You're going to drive everybody crazy."

"I really don't think so," said Sullivan. Manny, who was very thin and always wore a suit and tie and stood remarkably straight despite his age, had been standing in Sullivan's doorway. He still had his hair, which was now the color of ivory, and a little goatee — an empire, Manny called it. Sullivan had been sitting on the end of his bed, sulking. Having an eighty-one-year-old man as your friend was kind of neat, but having him as your closest friend wasn't neat. It was pathetic.

"Juggling would be just about the dorkiest thing I could do," Sullivan had said. "It would be like wearing a sign that said YES, I REALLY AM THAT BIG A LOSER. Besides, I'd be terrible at it. All I'd manage to do is drop things on my head."

And yet here he was, keeping four balls in the air at once. (Or so it looked. The balls were never actually all in the air at the same moment. There was always one in his hand, just caught or about to be thrown.)

"Sullivan!" came a voice from behind him. "I've already called three times. Now, please come for dinner."

The sound of his dad speaking made Sullivan miss a ball. The others rained down around him. Entering the room, his dad sighed as he helped pick them up. "Juggling again? Having a hobby is one thing, Sullivan. But having a hobby that interferes with your chores is another. You're keeping forty-eight hungry people waiting."

"Sorry, Dad. I guess I didn't hear you."

"And, Sullivan, put on some pants."

Sullivan placed the balls in the bottom drawer of his dresser. It used to be his sweater drawer, but he had moved the sweaters up one, cramming them in with his shirts. Now the drawer held all his juggling stuff — larger and smaller balls, clubs, plates, and instructional books. On his walls he had posters, not of baseball players or bands or movie stars, but of great jugglers of the past. There was Salerno, whose real name was Adolf Behrend and who was known as the "gentleman juggler" for dressing in tails and using hats and canes. There was Enrico Rastelli, maybe the greatest juggler of all time, who was known to practice constantly for the sheer love of it. There was the American Bobby May, who used comedy and was famous for his returning-bounce ball tricks. Sullivan even had a poster of ancient Egyptians juggling, from a painting inside a tomb. None of them had been easy to find. It wasn't as if you could walk into a poster shop and ask for the juggling section. He'd saved his small allowance and then ordered them from acrobatic supply companies that he found using the Internet at the public library.

Sullivan pushed the drawer closed and pulled on his cotton pants (his parents didn't like him to wear jeans at dinner). He was about to leave his room when something caught his eye through the window.

Sullivan moved over to it, put his hands on the sill, and leaned forward. There was something unusual moving down the street. It was dusk and the street-lights hadn't gone on yet, but in the gloom, moving past the worn-down houses on the other side, he could see a wagon. That would have been strange even if it wasn't being pulled by a horse. And it wasn't a wagon exactly, thought Sullivan. It was something else. A cara-van. Yes, that was the word. An old-fashioned wooden caravan, the likes of which he'd never seen before ex-cept maybe in pictures in some book.

The caravan had large wheels that turned slowly as the horse pulled it along. There was a sort of ornate carving around the top and sides. It looked like it be-longed in the time of western cowboy movies or in Vic-torian London. On the side, painted in fancy lettering, were the words *Master Melville's Medicine Show*. And under the arc of words was a picture of a narrow glass bottle with a stopper in it. Around the bottle were stars and lightning bolts.

It was only after he read the words that Sullivan noticed the figure on a seat at the front of the caravan, holding the horse's reins. The figure was hunched over and wore a big coat and a stovepipe hat. The face was hard to make out in the gloom, but Sullivan thought he saw a mustache and beard. There may have been somebody seated on the man's other side — he couldn't be sure.

The sight of the horse and driver and caravan was so strange that Sullivan felt as if he were looking backwards through time. But as he watched it pull out of sight, he heard another of his father's exasperated calls, and the spell was broken. He ran out of the room.

2

AN ANGRY MOB OF OLD FOGIES

SULLIVAN and his family lived on the top floor of a three-story house on the outskirts of the town of Beanfield. The other two floors made up the Stardust Home for Old People. To get to the dining room of the Stardust Home, Sullivan had to run along the hall and down two flights of stairs that creaked underfoot.

"Hurry up, Sullivan," said his mom. "Grab a tray." She rushed by, putting down hot dishes of breaded sole and cooked carrots and rice. A lot of the residents could eat only soft food, so most of the meals his father cooked—or rather, overcooked—were mushy. Sullivan hurried into the kitchen to load up a tray of his own. As he came out again, he saw a sheet of paper tacked to the bulletin board. He knew right away that his mother had written another poem. She wrote lots of poems, sometimes two or three a day, and she left them tacked on the board, or taped above the toilet in the bathroom, or pinned to a door. Once a week the local paper published one of her poems under the heading *The Bard of Beanfield*. But the residents of the Stardust Home were his mom's most devoted readers. Sullivan stopped a moment to read her latest.

I'll tell you then, I'll tell you now,
of all the beasts, I love the cow.
With eyes so pretty and breath so sweet,
she gives us both our milk and meat.

But I do feel bad, I must admit,
when into a burger I have bit
and I think I hear a call—but who?
Could it be the sound of "moo"?

No wonder they were having fish tonight. His tray loaded, Sullivan headed into the dining room. There were eight round tables covered in white cloths, each with six people—six white-haired or bald, liver-spotted people, some with trembling hands, others with watery eyes or shifting dentures—waiting for their dinner. It used to surprise Sullivan how eager old people were to get their dinner, even if they never ate very much, but by now he was used to it.

Sullivan went straight to table number seven, where Manny Morgenstern was talking to Elsa Fargo and Rita Cooley, two widowed sisters who always sat on either side of him.

"It's true. I really was a professional boxer," Manny was saying. "Of course, this was sixty years ago. My job was to lose and make my opponent look good. Which I was happy to do. Except for this one fight. You see, the five Trepovsky sisters came to see me. And I didn't want to look bad in front of them, because naturally, I was in love."

"But which of the Trepovsky sisters were you in love with?" asked Elsa.

"I can't remember. It was either sister number three or sister number five. My opponent was Hank 'the Crusher' Hopster and he looked like a gorilla, only he was hairier and uglier. I knew that my only chance was to surprise him with a knockout blow."

"And did you?" asked Rita breathlessly. "Did you knock him out?"

"I guess I wasn't as in love as I thought. I took one look at the Crusher, jumped over the rope, and ran out of the gym. I never boxed again. Instead, I got a job on a riverboat. Oh, Sullivan! I haven't seen you all day. What have you been working on?"

"Four balls," Sullivan said, putting down their plates.

"And?"

"Kept them up for twenty throws."

"Brilliant. You'd better keep serving or you'll have an angry mob of old fogies after you. Now, Elsa, Rita, did I ever tell you about the time I lived in Come By Chance, Newfoundland, testing rubber boots?"

Sullivan served two more tables and then sat down with his mother, his father (who was just taking off his apron), and his little sister, Jinny. "So how was school today?" his mom asked.

"Super great," said Jinny, who was only in first grade. "I made up a poem, just like you do. It's about a frog. Want to hear it?"

"No," said Sullivan. Jinny was always getting attention from their parents. It wasn't as if Sullivan wanted to be the center of attention, but still, it was annoying as anything. Now she was just sucking up to his poetry-loving mom.

"Of course we do. Go ahead," his mother said.

Jinny put her hands together and made her face look serious. She recited:

> A frog is the special-est thing in the world.
> More than a brother, a nail, or a bird.
> All the frogs love me, it really is true.
> But not brothers, because they smell like—

"Now that's enough, Jinny," his dad interrupted.

But Jinny insisted on shouting the last word out. "*Glue!*"

"Did anyone ever tell you that you're a genius, Jinny?" asked Sullivan. "Because if they did, they were lying."

His dad sighed. "Can we have some peace at the table, please? Otherwise I'll never be able to digest my food."

Sullivan's parents, Gilbert and Loretta, had been the managers of the Stardust Home for eight months. Before that they had run a diner, an old movie theater, a hair salon, and a beadery, and each time they had gone bankrupt. "Not," Sullivan's dad once admitted, "something to be really proud of." His parents worked hard, they got along with people, they always provided a good service. But the Mintzes just weren't competent at running a business. They paid too much for supplies and never charged enough for whatever they were selling. When people couldn't pay, they gave the meal (or the ticket, or the haircut, or the beads) away for nothing.

The Mintzes had hoped that the Stardust Home would be different. For one thing, they could save on expenses by living in the house themselves. For another, they could use the skills that they had learned running the other businesses. They could cook for all the residents, show movies and other entertainments in the evening, even cut hair and hold art workshops. They liked old people, who had so many fascinating stories to tell, and thought that it would be good for the children to be around them. And now that Sullivan was older, he was able to help a lot more.

But as always, things hadn't worked out as planned. For one thing, Sullivan's parents found running a home full of old people exhausting. There was a never-ending stream of chores—shopping, cooking, laundry, cleaning, pills to dispense, bored or lonely or irritable residents to cheer up, doctor's appointments to arrange. For another, Gilbert and Loretta seemed to attract people who had very small pensions or limited savings and could not afford to pay very much. In fact, if things continued on as they were now, the Stardust Home, like the other businesses, would soon go bankrupt. But this time, not only the Mintzes would suffer — all the residents would find themselves without a place to live.

Sullivan knew about these problems because he sometimes heard his parents talking at night when they thought he and Jinny were asleep. Sullivan was a natural worrier anyway. When he was five years old, he asked his parents what would happen if the sun didn't come up in the morning. When he was seven, he would look up at any airplane in the sky and watch until it passed over to make sure it didn't crash into their house. But the financial problems of the Stardust Home gave him something real to worry about. He would lie awake at night trying to come up with schemes that might help. He was too old to believe that a lemonade stand or selling all his comic books would be enough, as he used to think when his parents' other businesses were going under. But he wasn't too old to imagine he might earn enough money by juggling.

Was there some way that Sullivan could make money with his hobby? He couldn't remember ever seeing a juggler on television or in the movies. Maybe he could become a busker, one of those people who performs on a street corner or at a market while other people throw money into his hat. Sullivan would much rather be a busker than a dentist or accountant or any of the other things that his parents said were good careers. Could he make enough to help his family that way? And even if he could, was he good enough? Probably not. Not yet, anyhow. Even if he was, there was no way his parents would let him do that.

And then there was the little matter of stage fright.

For the truth was that Sullivan was seriously afraid of performing in front of people. Oh, he could juggle in front of his parents, or even Manny Morgenstern. But an audience—that was a different matter altogether. Just the thought of it made his hands sweat and his body begin to tremble. And yet the weird thing was that he *wanted* to perform for people. In fact, he wanted to so badly that it felt like something he would one day *have* to do. It was one of the things that kept him practicing every chance he got. But how could he ever perform, when he was terrified?

Sullivan's father pushed back his chair. "Showtime, folks," he said—it was what he always said when it was time to clear the plates and bring out dessert. When Sullivan reached Manny's table, his friend said to him, "So how about a little juggling for the old codgers tonight, Sullivan? I'm sure we could use some diversion."

Sullivan felt perspiration immediately spring to his forehead. "I've got a lot of homework," he said. "Maybe another time."

"That's what you always tell us," Elsa complained.

"Now, now," said Manny. "The boy has homework, didn't you hear? He'll juggle for us one day. When he's ready."

Good old Manny. Sullivan returned to his family's table to eat his own wedge of chocolate cake. His thoughts drifted back to the strange sight outside his window. Looking down at that caravan, he'd felt for a moment as if it were a hundred years ago. He had heard of medicine shows, but he wasn't exactly sure what they were. Then his thoughts were interrupted by his dad saying, "You'd better get down to that homework right after dinner. Your mom and I will do the dishes. When you're done, you can fold bed sheets. There's a mountain of them in the laundry room."

"Okay," Sullivan said. He didn't look forward to folding a zillion sheets. It was hard to get them properly square and flat. He hoped that he could finish the chore quickly enough to leave some time to practice before bed.

"I have homework, too," Jinny said.

"You're in first grade," Sullivan scoffed. "What homework do you have?"

"Coloring."

"Exactly."

"It's hard."

"I'm sure it is."

"Harder than learning Italian."

"I don't take Italian."

"It's still harder."

"Why are you talking to me, anyway?"

"Sullivan," said his dad. "Be nice to your sister."

"I'm the sort of person everybody just adores," said Jinny.

Sullivan rolled his eyes. He got up, took his plate into the kitchen, and went to do his homework.

THREE FACES

CROW gave a lonely caw and flew over the Stardust Home, past the last houses of the town, to a field that had not been plowed in years. The night was almost black, the moon and stars hidden by a dense layer of cloud. But the crow saw something down below that made it bank its wings and wheel in a circle. A horse was pulling a caravan over the uneven ground. The bird dropped lower, but then the man holding the horse's reins looked up and shook his fist. The crow flapped hard and pulled away.

The horse, clearly exhausted, breathed heavily and shook the bit in its mouth. "Come on, you mangy thing," said the man with the reins, and he cracked his whip against the horse's flank. "Don't give out on me yet. We're almost there."

The man wore a black stovepipe hat and a long black coat with the collar pulled up. A slighter figure next to him, sitting upright and wearing a hat ornamented with black feathers, was as unmoving as stone. The horse pulled the caravan along a stand of birch trees that stood ghostly in the dark, and the man pulled on the reins. "This'll do," he said. "We've gone far enough for tonight. Don't you think so, my dearest darling? I'm sure we've left that unfortunate little incident well behind."

"Cold," the other figure said. It was a woman's voice, breathy and shrill. "Damp. Uneven. Ugly. Yes, it'll do, you stupid excuse for a man. Next time let me pick the new talent. Now help me down."

"Of course, my sweet," the man said and he hurriedly jumped down, only to put his foot into a crumbling mound of old cow dung. But he said nothing, only came around to the other side of the caravan's seat, swung down a little wooden stair, and offered his hand. The woman took it with her own gloved hand and put one narrow, pointed black heel on the step.

Even in the dark her pale skin, shining black eyes, and ruby lips were visible.

"I'll get the urchins to make us a fire and a spot of late dinner, shall I?" the man said.

"Just make sure that no one has thoughts of running off."

"Oh, they all have thoughts of running, my dearest darling. Of course they do. But they *don't* run off. That's the thing. They wouldn't dare — I've seen to that. No need to worry your pretty head."

"Speak to me like that again and I'll take off your own head."

"Of course, my love. I well know who is the intelligence behind this enterprise. I assure you, I know that."

The man hurried to the back of the caravan, taking mincing steps in case there were any more cow patties. He took a large set of jangling keys from his inside pocket, found the one he needed, and slipped it into the padlock that secured the back door. He pulled on the lock, swung open the door, and, after taking a box from his outside pocket, struck a match.

The flame cast its feeble light into the caravan. Three young faces, eyes blinking, stared out. Dazed faces. Hungry faces.

"Don't just stare at me like a row of bobbleheads,"

said the man. "You know we had to pack up quick. Now Mistress and I want some dinner. And see to that worthless horse. Then it's back to bed. We've got a show tomorrow and I want you in good shape. Performances are getting slack. They've got to tighten up, do you hear? Now get on with it."

One by one the three children climbed out of the caravan. First a girl with long red hair, then a small boy, and last, an older boy. They did not speak, but, taking equipment from inside the caravan or strapped underneath or on top of it, they set up a cookstove, a table, folding chairs. The girl went to unharness the horse, whispering, "That's okay, that's all right" in its ear and patting its moist and shivering neck. The younger boy poured wine into two goblets, sniffling a little as if from a cold or perhaps holding back tears.

"I hate that noise," said the woman. "Make him stop."

"Of course, my buttercup." He stepped over to the boy and said, "You stop that right now. There's no need. Not when you're so well taken care of. Not when we've made your dreams come true. Hush up or there'll be no share for you and you can sleep on the ground under the caravan."

The man's voice sounded harsh, but he put his hand gently on the boy's shoulder. He took up the two goblets of wine and gave one to the woman. "Let us have a toast," he said. "To our great success!"

"Success?" the woman said. "You promised me the world. You promised me riches. Fame and glory. And look where we are. Look *what* we are. You are nothing but a disappointment to me."

"Ah, but things are looking up, my love. I sense a change in the air. I've got good instincts, and I can feel it!"

"Damn your instincts," she said, and swallowed her wine.

The older boy did the cooking. The sound of sizzling came from the stove, and the smell of oil, garlic, potatoes, and cheese made all three children painfully aware of their hunger. The woman said, "Well, I suppose you all need to eat as well. Let them get plates."

"You heard Mistress," said the man. "Go on now. And don't look so glum. We're all a little upset. But we'll be right as rain in a day or two. We'll be a jolly family once again. You'll see that I'm right!"

The girl brought out three more plates and the older boy served up the meal. The man and woman sat while the children stood. The horse pawed at the ground. "Yes," the man repeated, putting a forkful of hot potatoes into his mouth. "A jolly family once again."

4

TOMATO PANTS

Sullivan Mintz liked the Stardust Home better than any of the apartments they had rented in the past. Everyone was nice to him at the home. Even the most disagreeable resident, Dunstan Macafee — who complained that the food was too bland, that the other residents snored too loudly, and that the wallpaper looked like it was older than the residents — was nice to Sullivan. "Come over here, Sullivan," Mr. Macafee would call from his wheelchair. "Stand by the mark on the wall. Yes, I declare that you've grown at least an inch."

"I don't think I grew an inch since last week," Sullivan always said, for he knew that he wasn't growing very quickly at all and that Mr. Macafee was only trying to make him feel better.

"Don't disagree with me, young man. I was a tailor for fifty-seven years. I could eyeball a customer and tell you his exact height, not to mention his waist, seat, and inseam. And I say you're an inch taller."

Though everyone at the Stardust Home liked Sullivan, it was a different matter at Beanfield Middle School. Of course, the teachers were glad enough to have a student who did his work on time and never disrupted class. And he got along well enough with the other kids, even if he hadn't gotten to know many of them, since he could never go to their houses after school or stay for a club or dance. He had to hurry home and help his parents, something they took for granted, as if every kid had to help run the family business. But Sullivan's life at school was miserable. And for one reason.

Samuel Patinsky.

"Samuel Patinsky is a classic bully," said Norval Simick at lunch on Friday. Norval and Sullivan were friends, if you could call somebody you never saw outside of school a friend. They ate lunch together and tried to get picked for the same team in gym class, which wasn't always easy. Sullivan usually got picked somewhere in the middle, but Norval was always the last one chosen. To Sullivan the amazing thing was that Norval didn't mind. At least, Norval liked to say, he was known for *something*. And it was true, Sullivan thought. Nobody ever remembered who got picked in the middle.

"I don't know what you mean by 'classic,'" Sullivan said, looking suspiciously between the slices of bread of his sandwich. Usually his lunch consisted of whatever they'd had for dinner the night before, stuck between two pieces of pasty bread. Today it was a breaded sole sandwich.

"What I mean is that Samuel is a lunkhead, a dumb-bell, a cretin. He feels stupid and therefore bad about himself. He's also fat."

"He's not fat. He's just big."

"He's fat. And his parents fight all the time."

"How do you know that?"

"Wouldn't you fight if you were Samuel's parents?"

"So you're saying that I should feel sorry for Samuel Patinsky when he picks me up and shoves me inside my locker. When he pours my drink over my head. When he gives me a wedgie in gym. I should say, 'That's okay,

Sam, I know you have self-esteem issues. I hope torturing me makes you feel better.'"

"Pretty much."

"Hey, we've all got problems. I've got to serve forty-eight people dinner every night. Do you know how old they are if you add their ages together? I figured it out. *Three thousand eight hundred and seventy-three.* That's what *I* deal with every day."

"I thought you liked them."

"That's beside the point. I'm not going to feel bad for a Neanderthal like—"

"What are you gabbing about, Mr. Average?"

And there he was, Samuel Patinsky, playing a game on his cell phone even as he leaned over Sullivan and leered, his face as big as a pie. Sullivan could smell his breath. Peanut butter and onions.

"We were just having a fascinating discussion about recycling," said Norval in his most innocent voice. "Want to join in? Maybe you have an opinion about aluminum cans. And by the way, you're not supposed to use cell phones in school."

"Who was talking to you? I'll stick your head in a can if you don't shut up. So, Mintz," he said, turning back to Sullivan. "Guess what my mother put in my lunch today?"

"I don't know."

Samuel had a paper bag tucked under his arm. He reached into it and pulled out three small tomatoes. He held them up so that they were almost touching Sullivan's nose.

"Very nice," said Sullivan.

"No, not very nice. I hate tomatoes." He put them down on the table. "They're like eating the inside of a frog. I'm trying to decide what to do with them. You have any ideas?"

Norval leaned close to Sullivan's ear. "Now's your chance. Juggle the tomatoes. You'll amaze him. You'll amaze everybody in the cafeteria."

Norval knew about Sullivan's interest in juggling, just as Sullivan knew that Norval was into model rocketry. But Norval had never actually seen Sullivan juggle. Sullivan always said he would show him another time.

"What are you whispering about?" asked Samuel.

Sullivan picked up the three tomatoes. He felt them in his hands. They weren't too ripe and might not break if he tossed them carefully.

He put them back on the table.

"Sorry. I can't think of a thing to do with them."

"Then I guess I'll have to figure out something myself. Wait, I've got it! Stand up, Mintz."

"I'm not finished with my lunch."

"I said, stand up."

Sullivan stood up. He watched as Samuel picked up the tomatoes and put them down on the seat of Sullivan's chair.

"Sit down again."

"I don't think that's a good idea."

"Sit *down*."

Sullivan lowered himself carefully. Then Samuel grabbed him by the shoulders and pushed him down, hard, into the seat.

"That can't feel very nice," Norval said, making a face.

It didn't feel nice. But Sullivan didn't say anything. He couldn't think of anything clever—in fact, he was holding back tears. "Have a great day, Tomato Pants!" said Samuel, walking away. Sullivan's shoulders slumped and his head lowered almost to his chest. Norval started saying something to him, but he didn't hear a thing.

It is a sad truth that all too often the victims of people like Samuel Patinsky keep it a secret. Sullivan had considered telling his parents; in fact, he'd been on the verge of telling them several times. But something always came up. Last time it was Jinny insisting they all sit down and watch her pretend to be a sunflower opening up to the sun. And even if his parents did have a moment, Sullivan believed that they wouldn't really listen to him. "That's nice," they would say, no matter what he told them, "and by the way, did you empty everybody's trash can? And water the plants? And take those eight bags of shrimp out of the basement freezer?" Anyway, what would he say this time, that Samuel Patinsky made him sit on some tomatoes? If his parents complained, the whole school would learn about it. Most of them wouldn't even know who he was, but then kids would start pointing him out. They'd all start calling him Tomato Pants, which was even worse than Mr. Average.

At least, that was what he believed would happen. The reality was that Sullivan was not the only boy being bullied by Samuel. If he had told, as Norval often encouraged him to, he would have found himself with several new friends and general gratitude from the student population.

❋

Norval had a pair of sweatpants in his locker and lent them to Sullivan. At home after school, Sullivan threw his own pants into the laundry and then began his chores. He sorted the mail and delivered it to the residents in their rooms, politely chatting with each. He got Jinny a snack of crackers and jam because his father was out food shopping and his mother was at the bank talking to the manager again. (Jinny complained that he didn't use enough jam.) He emptied wastepaper baskets in the common rooms. Only then could he finally do what he was longing to, the one thing that helped him to forget about Samuel Patinsky and about how his parents never listened and that he was so uninteresting and average that nobody even knew who he was.

Taking three balls from his drawer, Sullivan began a regular cascade, the balls weaving past each other in the air. He switched to a shower, with the balls chasing one another up and down again. He paused — one ball balanced on his arm, one on his shoulder, and one on his foot. Then he tossed a ball up with his foot and set them all in motion again.

Over the shoulder. Under the leg. Over the arm. Behind the back. Then a column, with two balls tossed straight up with one hand and a third ball with the other. He caught them, added a fourth ball, began again, dropped a ball, began again, dropped a ball again, began once more. When he dropped two balls he threw them all into the drawer and took out his wooden clubs.

At first he had found using clubs especially hard. Just the idea of throwing them up into the air and trying to catch them scared him. Unlike balls, clubs had to turn just the right number of times so that they came down with their handles facing him. The smack when they met his hands stung. Even though he'd gotten better, he was still afraid of conking himself on the head.

He got the three clubs into an easy pattern and then threw them higher. The ceiling was covered in scuff marks from throws that were too high. He wanted to try a 360-degree spin, whipping around in a circle before catching the clubs again. But he was a split second slow and they rained down on him. "Ow!" he cried, protecting himself with his arms. When he looked up, he saw Manny Morgenstern watching from the doorway.

"Did you have to witness that particular moment?" asked Sullivan.

Manny said, "When you mess up, it's a sign of progress. I once saw a juggler in a vaudeville theater back in the old days. He juggled three clubs while going up and down a flight of stairs on a unicycle. It took him months to learn how to do it."

Sullivan put his clubs away in the drawer. "What was vaudeville like?" he asked.

"Of course, I didn't see vaudeville in its heyday. It was already dying out. What was it like? You would go to the theater and buy a ticket—you could go in any time of the afternoon or evening because it didn't really have a beginning or an end. Just one act after another, all day long. You might see a comedian, a juggler, a bunch of clowns, a lady singer, a short play, a snake act. There was a little orchestra of four or five musicians playing the popular tunes of the day and also the music for the acts. It was great, it was lousy, it was silly, it was funny . . . it was always changing. I loved it. Of course, I loved all kinds of performances. Dramatic plays, musical comedies. The circus, when it came into town. If it was on a stage, any stage, I tried to see it."

Sullivan asked, "Did you ever see a medicine show?"

Manny rubbed his little goatee while he thought. "No, I don't believe I did. But I've heard of them. They're long gone, died out even before vaudeville. I bet there hasn't been a medicine show for seventy or eighty years."

"What are—I mean, what *were* they?"

"A kind of traveling show, I suppose. Often with a wagon that went from town to town, or village to village, the small places that didn't get regular theater shows. They'd set up a little stage and have some kind of act—singing, dancing, mind-reading, banjo playing, you name it. And of course there was the pitchman."

"The pitchman?"

Manny didn't seem to hear him. "I suppose it was

phonographs and radio and the movies that killed off medicine shows, just like they did vaudeville. And they'll never come back. Nowadays people are used to special effects, light shows, 3D, watching images on big screens and tiny screens, all kinds of nonsense. But that was some entertainment, Sullivan. That was the real thing. People performing right before your eyes."

Sullivan had a lot more questions for Manny, but at that moment he heard his mother calling for him to come and help set the tables for dinner.

"I'll give you a hand," Manny said. "I hear it's fried chicken tonight. I just live for that fried chicken. Which is funny when you consider that the chicken died for it. Listen, Sullivan—I've got a thought. How about you put on a little juggling show for the residents after dinner tonight? I'm sure they'd love it."

Manny made the suggestion as if it were the first time, as if he didn't make it every day. Sullivan hesitated. Every night he lay in bed and imagined performing for people, but the chance to actually do it made him turn ice cold. "I don't think I'm ready yet," he said. "Soon, though."

"Whatever you say. But don't wait for perfection, Sullivan. Or you'll be waiting a very long time, I'm afraid."

✻

Only later in the evening, after dinner was cleared away and the residents had moved on to playing cards or listening to music or watching television or visiting with their relatives or sitting in their rooms doing nothing at all, did the Mintz family get some quiet time. They sat in their small third-floor sitting room with the castoff sofa and armchairs and a fireplace that didn't work. Sullivan's dad found that knitting helped him relax at the end of the day, and he was working on a sweater for Jinny. Sullivan's mom sat at a small desk with the account books open before her. Sullivan sat on the other side of the desk, doing his homework. Jinny was lying on the rug, looking at some picture books from the library.

"I don't know how we're going to keep this place running past the end of the year," his mom said, as if she had forgotten the children were present. Unless, Sullivan considered, she was trying to prepare them, which meant that the situation was even worse than he had thought. "The man at the bank says he can't loan us another cent without permission from the head office."

"Perhaps we could think about it another night."

"Gilbert, you always say that. And then we go bankrupt."

"It's a good point, dear. I do always say that. Jinny,

stand up so I can put this sweater against you and see how it's going to fit."

Jinny stood up and held out her arms. "I could make lots of money," Jinny offered.

"You could?" said her dad, checking the sleeve length. "Well, that's just wonderful. And how will you make lots of money?"

"That's easy. I'll find treasure."

"A fantastic idea. And how will you find treasure?"

"Oh, that's easy, too, Daddy. You can bury it and I'll find it."

"Now, why didn't I think of that?"

Sullivan got up from the desk and looked out the window. There was nobody outside, only a broken chair by the curb across the road. At least his sister had an idea, he thought, even if it was one that made no sense. Sullivan wished again that he could find a way to bring in money. If he could only get over his fear of performing in front of people, maybe he really could make money juggling. Maybe he could join a circus. They still existed, didn't they?

"The mood is far too gloomy in here," his dad said. "Sullivan, why don't you take Jinny for a walk to the corner store. You can get yourselves a treat."

"It worked!" Jinny cried. "I was thinking, *Let us have*

a treat, let us have a treat. I sent my brain message to you."

Sullivan said, "Mom and Dad let us get a treat lots of nights."

"Well, I for one think it's amazing," his dad said. "Keep an eye on your sister, Sullivan."

"Oh, he will," said Jinny. "'Cause he *loooves* me."

"Dream on, sis."

His dad fished around in his pocket and came up with four quarters. Sullivan put them in his own pocket. A dollar wasn't going to buy them much of a treat. He wished that he could be more like Jinny. He wished a treat made everything wonderful for him, too.

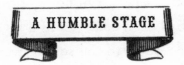

* 5 *

A HUMBLE STAGE

THE Stardust Home had once been owned by the richest family in Beanfield. They had owned the sawmill and the undergarment factory and the newspaper. On a local history website, Sullivan had seen an old photograph of it as it had been back then—prettily painted, with a fine manicured lawn and men in top hats and women with parasols strolling about or sitting on the veranda. It had been built on the outskirts of town, and Beanfield hadn't grown much since then. There were still farms and fields behind the now rundown house. The little store that Sullivan and Jinny walked to was the very last building in town.

Yesterday had been cold, but as if by some miracle, Sullivan stepped out into the sort of fresh spring evening that made him feel that something good, even extraordinary, was going to happen; something that he couldn't possibly guess. He breathed the sweet air and saw how the sun was already low between the distant houses.

"You need to hold my hand," Jinny insisted.

"Ugh, your hand is sticky. I don't need to hold it. I can see that you're right beside me."

"Okay, I'll lick it all over. Yum-yum-yum. There. It isn't sticky anymore. You can hold it now."

"That's worse! Give me your other hand, at least."

None of the other houses on the street were anywhere near as large as the Stardust Home, but they were all nearly as old. They were also poorly kept up, in need of paint, mortar between the flaking bricks, and porch repairs. Sullivan saw a blind go down in a second-floor window and a cat stretch itself on a sagging porch chair before closing its eyes again. A breeze came up and stirred the leaves on the big trees. It made a newspaper flutter down the road and a Styrofoam cup roll and bounce. A long and narrow sheet of paper did a loop in the air, skittered along the sidewalk, and plastered itself against Sullivan's legs.

He leaned down and peeled the paper off, then held it up.

— MEN, WOMEN, BOYS, GIRLS! —
Step back in time and see the one and only
MASTER MELVILLE'S MEDICINE SHOW
Witness the mystifying conjuring effects of
✱ FREDERICK, the Boy Wonder!
Gasp at the mind-boggling intelligence of
✱ NAPOLEON, the Chess-Playing Automaton!
Roar with delight at the antics of
✱ SNIT & SNOOT, the World's Worst-Trained Dogs!
Swoon at the sheer poetry of
✱ ESMERALDA, Angel of the Air!
And the cost to you? Absolutely nothing!
Sunset, south end of Reingold's Field
⌒ PLAYING NOW! ⌒

"Let me see it, let me see it!" Jinny said.

"You can't even read." Sullivan kept his eyes on the paper.

"Then what does it say?"

"It's some sort of show."

"Oh, goody. When is it?"

"It says at sunset, over in Reingold's Field. That's just about now."

"Let's go! Let's go!" Jinny started pulling at Sullivan's shirt.

"Stop that. This could be from yesterday, or a month or a year ago."

"But it isn't! It's now! It says right on it. Let's go, Sullivan!"

Sullivan shrugged. Yet he, too, was excited by the chance of seeing a show. The name — Master Melville — was the same as on the caravan from the night before. Reingold's Field wasn't far past the store. Sometimes kids played ball games there, although all Sullivan ever did was watch from the side. There couldn't be any harm in going just to see. He took Jinny's hand and began walking quickly. They passed the store and kept going to the end of the sidewalk and through the first open field where an old barn stood, its roof collapsed.

A barbed wire fence ran along the border of the next field, but it had fallen down in several places so it was easy for them to step over. Weeds and stray grasses and wildflowers grew along the old furrows. There was a creek on one side, and along it a billboard had been planted into the ground with wooden stakes. COMING

Past it a line of trees began, and beyond them Sullivan could see a small crowd of people.

"There it is!" he cried. "Let's hurry." He began to run, pulling Jinny after him. He caught his foot in a groundhog hole and almost fell, but picked himself up again. Jinny began to cry that she couldn't go so fast, so he put his arm around her and half carried her the last stretch.

They joined the small crowd of thirty or so people, their backs to Sullivan and Jinny as they faced the side of the caravan. And yes, it was definitely the same caravan that Sullivan had seen on the street the night before. So there really was still a medicine show, even if they were supposed to have been long gone. Could this be the extraordinary thing that he had felt in the spring air?

He didn't recognize any of the people in the crowd. They must have been from the nearby farms or from houses whose kids went to the school in the next district. It wasn't like Sullivan to be pushy, but he was so eager to see the show that he held Jinny's hand and worked his way to the front.

He could see that the long wooden side of the caravan had been let down to form a sort of stage. There was a curtain painted with a scene of green hills and a distant, ancient city in ruins. A kerosene lantern hanging on either side cast a yellow light.

Jinny, who had been hopping from one foot to the other in anticipation, slowly grew still. She grasped the edge of Sullivan's shirt with her fingers. "Sullivan?" she said. "Maybe we should go home. I don't like it here. And it's getting dark."

"What do you mean? This could be good."

"It feels funny."

"What are you talking about? Shhh. The show's going to start."

Sullivan heard a rhythmic beating. From around the side of the caravan came a woman dressed in black, her face slim and pale and beautiful, her lips a deep red. She had a big bass drum strapped to her back; a washboard and cowbells on her front; a banjo-ukulele in her hands; a metal contraption holding a harmonica, a kazoo, and a whistle before her mouth; and a cymbal on a little shoulder perch. As she walked, a rope on her foot made the bass drum boom, while on her other ankle a tambourine rattled. She began to strum the banjo-ukulele while buzzing the jazzy melody of "Five Foot Two, Eyes of Blue" on the kazoo, her cheeks puffing out. Sullivan knew the song because Manny liked to hum it.

And then a cymbal crash and silence. At that same

moment the curtain was pushed aside and a very tall, very thin man came out. His face was gaunt, his pock-marked cheeks visible through his scraggly beard, eyebrows heavy and eyes quick and shining. He wore a suit that was not black, as Sullivan had thought looking through the window the night before, but rather a deep purple, with yellow stitching and a waistcoat beneath the jacket that was a wild paisley of gold and red. The silk scarf knotted about his neck was green. He removed his stovepipe hat and made an exaggerated bow.

"Dear friends," the man said. "Yes, although we have not met, I consider each and every one of you a friend. For are we not all sons of Adam and daughters of Eve, all part of one family?"

A honk from the side of the stage. Sullivan looked over to see the woman who made the music holding up a bicycle horn and scowling.

"But I get carried away," he said, stroking his thin beard. "It is excitement, sheer excitement over what we shall offer you good people this evening. A show, certainly, but not just any show. For we have gathered together, on this humble stage, a band of uniquely talented *artistes*. Performers who, although tender in years and fresh of face, have already reached the pinnacle of their particular *métiers*. Each one of them could have already found fame and fortune on the greatest stages of the world — in London, Paris, or New York. Yet they have all chosen to dedicate themselves to an older and more intimate form of theatrical expression. That is" — the man motioned to the curtain behind him — "to the small stage of a traveling show. They have only their honest talents to hold your attention."

The man lowered his head a moment and cleared his throat with an awful rumble. He looked up again. "But I know that you are all eager for the show to begin. Dear friends, my name is Montague Melchior Melville — Master Melville, as my colleagues in the impresario trade have declared me out of deep respect. And that divine creature to my left," he said, gesturing to the woman bound in musical instruments, "that vision of loveliness is the one dearest to my heart. My own wife, Mistress Eudora Melville, is a woman of most sprightly melodic agility."

Master Melville looked at the woman as if expecting her to thump her drum or strum her banjo-ukulele or toot something in recognition of his compliment. But she merely continued to examine the edges of her long, painted fingernails. So he said, "Let me please insist that the taking of photographs or videos is strictly forbidden. No cameras, no cell phones, no modern geegaws or what-do-you-call-its of any kind. Each of our performances is meant to exist only for the moment and then in the golden haze of memory, like the wondrous shows of old." Several people put away their phones. "Much obliged. And now let me introduce the first act. Rest assured, I will be back. For I have a message for you all. A message that could make all the difference to each and every one of you . . . that may mean the difference between a life of misery and a life of bliss."

Jinny tugged again at Sullivan's shirt. "He sure talks a lot."

Sullivan ignored her. "But enough for now," Master Melville went on. "Without further delay, I give you a boy on the brink of manhood, who not long ago shaved the fuzz from his upper lip for the first time. And yet he is a conjurer so masterful that the famous magicians of our time have fallen at his feet, begging for his secrets. Ladies and gentlemen, you are about to be astonished, astounded, and awestruck. For I give you . . . *Frederick, the Boy Wonder!*"

With a flourish of his hand, Master Melville commanded the curtain to open. Mistress Melville began to play a jerky waltz. The curtain started to move, got stuck, and then flew to the sides to reveal a boy of thirteen or fourteen with blond hair sticking out from under his black silk hat. He looked uncomfortable in a tuxedo that had been turned up at the trouser cuffs and sleeves. He gazed at the audience without smiling, as if, thought Sullivan, he was mad at them all just for being there.

"I'm supposed to entertain you," the boy said. "Only I forgot to bring any playing cards. That's how much I care. But I don't have much choice, since you're here, so I'll just have to get some. Of course to do that I need to make a door. Let's see. Up here looks like a good place."

The boy stretched out his hand and with a finger he traced a square in the air just higher than his head. Then he pretended to grasp an invisible knob and open the door. "All I need to do now," he said, "is take what I want." He raised his hand again and reached "through" the door, and as he pulled it back a playing card instantly appeared in his hand. He held it out for the audience to see. Then he took off his hat, dropped the card in, and reached through the door again. He snatched another card from the air and dropped it into the hat. He did it again and again, one card after another, until he had at least a dozen.

"That ought to be enough," the boy said. He picked all the cards out of the hat and put the hat back on. He fanned them out to show their faces — they were all red — and then waved them through the air, turning them black. He passed them *through* his hat. He threw one into the air, where it vanished, only to appear in his pocket. He tore one to bits, swallowed the pieces, then drew it out of his mouth whole again. He dropped the cards into his upturned hat and fluttered his fingers over them, coaxing them to float into the air one after another. And after they dropped back into the hat, he picked them up one at a time, reached through the invisible doorway in the air, and made each one vanish again.

The crowd clapped and whistled.

"I'm bored of doing this," the boy said. "I don't give a hoot what you think. But I'll do one more because I feel like it. I'll try something different, something I've never done before. You see, even though I'm still a kid, I'm going to buy my first house."

A few titters from the crowd. Sullivan looked down for a moment to see Jinny staring expectantly at the boy on stage. He continued, "The problem is, the house I want to buy is haunted."

"Haunted?" whispered Jinny.

"Let me show you the house. I've got it here."

The boy, Frederick, went to the side of the stage and brought out a giant sheet of cardboard with the simple front of a house drawn on it. The audience laughed. He brought out another sheet meant to be the side of the house and he propped the two together. He brought out a third and a fourth sheet, making a sort of cardboard play house. Sullivan looked down at Jinny again and saw that she wasn't scared; she was smiling. He knew what she was thinking—that it would be fun to play inside the cardboard house.

"To get the ghost out of the house I'm going to have to trick him," said Frederick. "But first I'm going to have to make him think I'm another ghost."

The boy went to the side of the stage again and this time he came back with a rolled-up sheet. He unrolled it and showed the crowd that there were two small holes cut in the center. Sullivan knew they were eye holes, and sure enough the boy draped the sheet over himself to become a Halloween ghost.

"Not bad," Frederick said, holding out his arms and turning around. "Now all the house needs is the roof." He walked once more to the side of the stage, this time coming back with a sheet of cardboard that was bent down the middle to have a peak like a roof. He lowered it onto the walls.

But as soon as the roof was on the house a terrible moaning and groaning came from inside. Then knocks and screams and the sound of breaking glass. Had the ghost inside become angry? Jinny grabbed Sullivan's arm and held it tight. Sullivan himself wasn't scared, not really, and he couldn't stop watching.

The boy slowly picked up the roof again.

As he did so the ghost in the house — or at least somebody in another bed sheet costume — rose up, too. The boy put down the roof, grabbed the ghost's sheet, and pulled it off.

And underneath the sheet was . . . *the boy!*

But how could that be? Frederick, the boy magician, was the one *outside* the house! Sullivan couldn't understand. Were they identical twins? The boy standing inside the house now grabbed the sheet of the ghost outside the house and pulled *it* off.

And underneath was . . . *a girl!* Not the magician at all, but a girl maybe twelve years old, with long red hair and freckles, wearing a white satin gown. How had the boy ended up in the house? How had the girl ended up where the boy had been? It really was amazing. Sullivan pulled his arm from Jinny's grasp so he could join the enthusiastic clapping of the crowd.

The curtain closed — from his spot near the stage, Sullivan could hear it creaking. The woman in black, Mistress Melville, boomed the drum, crashed the cymbal, and began a military march, her arms flailing at the banjo-ukulele, her legs pumping up and down to keep the drum and tambourine going, her mouth blowing into the whistle. Out stepped Master Melville, grinning and nodding.

"Wonderful, just wonderful," he said. "If only the lad would smile, but you know how moody kids are at that age. And what an attitude! If he were to take some of these drops, his disposition would improve immediately, I assure you."

From his inside pocket, Master Melville pulled out a small glass bottle with a paper label and a stopper in its neck. It looked like the same kind of bottle Sullivan had seen painted on the side of the caravan the night before. "Yes," the tall man went on, holding it up. "If he would only take a daily dose of Master Melville's Hop-Hop Drops, young Frederick would be smiling away. Certified organistic, one hundred percent anti-parsinomic, Master Melville's Hop-Hop Drops are just the thing when life's got you down. They are like nothing you can buy from a pharmacy or get from a doctor's prescription. They are all natural, they disperse all acidity and acrimony from the bloodstream, they facilitate remification and inhibit ramification. And they are guaranteed—guaranteed right on the bottle—to make you a happier person."

Master Melville took in a deep breath and smiled warmly as he looked around. Sullivan felt for a moment that Master Melville was looking not just at him but *through* him. "But let me tell you about these miraculous drops later. I'm sure you would like to see our next performer. Although, to tell you the truth, I don't know if I can call *it* a performer at all. Ladies and gentlemen, allow me to present to you the most astonishing piece of machinery ever produced by humankind. Over two hundred years old, it is run by the simple mechanistic laws of cogs and wheels, springs and screws. And yet, it can think. It can reason. And it can win. Introducing the Chess-Playing Genius . . . *Napoleon!*"

Once more the curtain opened, showing the bare stage. A moment later Frederick the magician wheeled out a strange object. It was a figure, or more precisely the top half of a figure, sitting on a low wooden cabinet. A sort of model or mannequin, it had a painted wooden head that looked a little like Napoleon the French emperor, and it was wearing a tricorn hat, a red and blue military jacket, and white gloves.

"Yes, ladies and gentlemen," Master Melville continued as he walked over to the figure, "Napoleon plays an amazing game of chess. It has defeated Russian grandmasters and French champions. It has amazed kings and queens in courts all over Europe. And it is nothing but clockwork inside. Let me show you."

Master Melville opened a little door in the front

of the cabinet. Inside, Sullivan could see wheels and gears, a rubber belt, and a metal cylinder with little studs on it like the workings of a music box. Then the man and the young magician turned the cabinet around on its wheels and opened the back door to show more wheels and cogs and springs. "You see? There are no wires or chips, no twenty-first-century electronic thingamajigs. Only what you'd find on the inside of your grandfa-ther's watch. Indeed, it was constructed by a watch-maker of the old school. But his secrets died with him, and now only one such automaton exists. For years it was believed lost forever, but after a lifetime of search-ing, I found it — where, I cannot say."

Frederick and Master Melville turned the automa-ton to the front again, and as the magician left the stage, Master Melville opened a drawer at the bottom of the cabinet and took out a set of black and white chess pieces. He placed them on a board that lay on the cabinet in front of Napoleon.

"Is there by any chance a chess player in the crowd? Someone adept at this ancient game that requires deep thinking? Don't be shy now — here is your chance to show off before all these good people."

Sullivan waited. After a moment a man in overalls, a baseball cap on his head, stepped forward. "I'm par-tial to a game of chess," he said.

"You're good, too," said the woman behind him. "Nobody around here can beat you."

"Then you are just our man!" said Master Melville. "Would you like to play Napoleon?"

"Don't mind if I do."

"Excellent. All I need to do is wake it up."

Master Melville pulled from inside his jacket a set of keys. He went to the side of the cabinet, inserted a key, and with much effort began to wind up the automaton. There was a noise of whirs and gears and then the wooden head turned to the left, the right, and back again. The left hand of the figure lurched upward. It moved forward and the fingers opened to pinch the top of a pawn. It placed the pawn two squares forward and lurched back again.

"Your turn, if you please," Master Melville said to the man, holding out a hand to help him onto the stage.

Sullivan wasn't much for games, and he was a poor chess player. But he found it intensely interesting to watch the man play against the machine. Even Jinny, who didn't understand chess, watched with rapt attention. The man in the baseball cap would move a piece. Then a whirring sound would come from Napoleon and its wooden eyeballs would move back and forth as if it were thinking. Its arm would lurch forward again to make its move. The whole audience watched in silence. Napoleon picked up a bishop and moved it across the board to knock over the man's king. Bells and whistles sounded inside the automaton and the left hand pinched the three-cornered hat and raised it off the wooden head and back down.

"Checkmate!" cried Master Melville. "Napoleon wins!"

Everyone clapped except for the man in the baseball cap, who sheepishly slipped off the stage. The curtain closed, the clanging music started up (a polka this time, with harmonica), and Master Melville stood before the audience once more. "Oh, dear," he said. "Nobody likes to lose, especially to a pile of junk. But if this gentleman would only take a sip from a bottle of my Hop-Hop Drops, his mood would change in moments. The world would look sunny and bright again. That, my dear friends, is the natural effect of this remarkable infusion.

"Ladies and gentlemen," Master Melville went on, "modern medicine is a wonder. I do not denigrate our doctors, our hospitals with their beeping machines, our X-rays and laser surgeries, our capsules and injections. And yet there is much that the wise healers of the past can teach us. Perhaps you can't sleep since your teenage son ran away. Or you feel worthless for having lost your job. Or you suspect that the person you married twenty years ago no longer loves you. Can modern medicine cure any of these ailments?

"The drops in this bottle" — again he pulled it from his pocket — "are a very old concoction, once known to the ancient Egyptians, then to the great healers of the Mayan civilization, and last to the Chinese of the Ming Dynasty. A recipe lost for generations until discovered by myself in a musty tome and refreshed and revitalized with the addition of certain modern ingredients to make it even more powerful. Ingredients, to be frank, that are available to each and every one of you in the corner grocery store, the field and the stream. But what are they and in what combination? How are they prepared? That, friends, is the secret that I hold. And that I keep to myself for fear of misuse and malevolence. Why, I'm so confident in these drops that I shall give a bottle away for free to the man who went down to defeat only moments ago. Here you go, sir!"

And with that Master Melville tossed the bottle into the air. There were chuckles as the man in the baseball cap caught it. He looked embarrassed, but he slipped the bottle into the big pocket of his overalls.

At that moment Mistress Melville struck up a lively tune, bashing on her instruments and blowing hard into the kazoo. Master Melville began to dance. He lifted his arms, rose on his toes, and kicked out one leg as he spun around.

"Sullivan! We have to go." Jinny began smacking her brother on the back with her hands.

"Ow! Stop that."

"Mom and Dad are going to wonder where we are. It's dark. I don't like walking in the dark."

Sullivan had to admit that Jinny was right. Their parents were going to start worrying. He hated the idea of not being able to see the rest of the show, but there didn't seem to be anything else to do. "All right," he said, grabbing Jinny's wrist. He began to pull her aside, out of the crowd.

When he looked up he saw the woman, Mistress Melville, her arms pumping wildly as she played her instruments. She was already looking at him — looking straight at him with such intensity that he silently gulped. She took her mouth off the kazoo and said, "You, boy. I have a feeling about you. Come back tomorrow."

"Tomorrow?" Sullivan said, astonished.

But she was looking at the stage again, strumming furiously on the banjo-ukulele and swinging her leg to bang the drum.

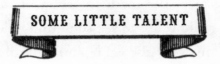

SOME LITTLE TALENT

ᛏHE town of Beanfield got its name for a good reason: almost all the surrounding farmers grew beans. The importance of beans to the economy of the town wasn't lost on Beanfield Middle School. Every year there was a special presentation in the gym. The morning after Sullivan and Jinny's trip to the medicine show, they sat with their classes and watched a PowerPoint presentation called "Is the Bean the Greatest Vegetable Ever?"

Sullivan could hardly concentrate on the screen, or

on any of his classes afterward, for his mind whirled with memories of the medicine show. It was as if he'd been waiting all his life to see something like it, maybe even to see this very show. He could hardly wait to go again tonight. The woman herself had invited him!

After school, Sullivan had his usual chores, and after dinner, too. Then he went to find Jinny, who was in her room posing in front of the mirror in a pair of her mother's high-heeled shoes and singing at the top of her lungs.

I'm a great singer and dancer too!

Also a great swimmer, pole vaulter, piano player, gum chewer —

"Hey, Jinny," Sullivan interrupted. "Mom asked me to read some stories to you tonight. But I want to go back to the medicine show. How about you look at some picture books by yourself?"

"Nope."

"Please?"

"Only if you play with me now."

"I'll play anything you want."

"Okay, let's play Baddy-Waddy Widdle Boy."

Sullivan groaned. "I hate that game."

"You said *anything*."

"Fine."

"Yes!" Jinny cried.

And so for the next hour they played Baddy-Waddy Widdle Boy. Jinny was the school teacher, Miss Mintz, and Sullivan was the boy who was always getting into trouble. He didn't do his homework, he didn't listen, he never knew the answer when Miss Mintz called him to the blackboard. Naturally there were, as Miss Mintz said with exasperation, "con-see-quences." He had to stand on one leg in the corner. He had to write "I'm a Baddy-Waddy Widdle Boy" a hundred times on the blackboard. He had to answer questions like "What happens when you mix dishwashing soap with rocket fuel?"

Finally Sullivan broke away to find his parents in the sitting room. His father was knitting, his mother, with her notebook in her lap, was writing a new poem. Sullivan hesitated, for it wasn't like him to outright lie to his parents. He forced himself to speak quickly.

"So I was thinking of putting Jinny to bed myself."

His parents looked up. "You mean you're offering?" asked his dad.

"I thought, you know, that it would be good for us. Bonding. Jinny wants me to. Is that okay?"

His parents looked at each other. "That will be a first," his mom said. "Sure. It's really nice of you, Sullivan. You're a wonderful big brother."

Sullivan wished his mother hadn't said that. He

turned around and went back to Jinny in her room. She was sitting on the edge of the bed, waiting for him.

"Aren't we going to play some more?"

"No, I have to go. The medicine show must have already started. You can look at your books now."

"I changed my mind. I want to go with you."

"Come on, Jinny. It's late. And dark outside."

"I can bring my Super-Explorer flashlight."

"All right, but you can't tell Mom and Dad. And hurry."

Sullivan had to wait while Jinny hunted for the flashlight. Then they crept along the hall and down the stairs to the ground floor. All the residents were in their rooms and the living room lights were off. The furniture cast long shadows in the dark. Suddenly, a light right in Sullivan's eyes blinded him.

"Hey, what are you doing?"

"You said I could use my flashlight."

"Outside! And don't point it in my face."

Slowly, Sullivan opened the door and they slipped out. Jinny turned her flashlight back on and pointed it at the ground as they began walking.

"Is this an adventure?" Jinny asked.

"You don't have to whisper anymore. And yes, it's an adventure."

"Good, because I always wanted one."

They didn't speak much as they continued to walk, past the store and then the abandoned barn, over the barbed wire fence and past the creek to Reingold's Field.

"There they are," Jinny said, although Sullivan had already seen the people gathered just past the trees. A glow came from the lamps on either side of the caravan stage and the music drifted toward them. They walked more quickly now, half running until they reached the back of the crowd, which was smaller this time. Sullivan tried to move them forward but could only get to the side. Master Melville was dancing just as he'd been when they'd left the night before. He did one more turn and stopped.

"But you haven't come to watch me do a jig!" the tall man said breathlessly. "Let me introduce our next act, Clarence and his incorrigible canines *Snit* and *Snoot,* the World's Worst-Trained Dogs!"

The music galloped on as Master Melville danced himself off the stage. Then the woman in black began another tune, one that Sullivan recognized as "How Much Is That Doggy in the Window?" This time the curtain opened very slowly to show a small boy standing between two even smaller dogs. The boy had straight bangs across his forehead and large eyes, and wore *lederhosen*—leather shorts—with suspenders.

The two dogs were white with dark patches and had little tails and small ears that flopped down. Jinny was making noises about how cute they were.

"Hello, everyone," said the boy, giving a little wave. "Tonight I'm supposed to present a dog act. There have been many great dog acts. Unfortunately, this isn't one of them. That's because the two dogs here, Snit and Snoot, won't do anything I say. For example, they won't ever jump——"

At that moment the dog on the boy's right side did jump——right over his head! But the boy didn't seem to notice. He went on, "——or do anything I ask. It would be nice if they listened to me once in a while and jumped when I asked them."

The dog on the left jumped over him. Again, the boy didn't seem to notice. It barked and wagged its tail. The boy looked at the dog and just shook his head.

"Let me give you an example. Watch this. Okay, Snit and Snoot. Roll over!"

The two little dogs stood up on their hind legs. They walked in little tippy-toe circles.

"See what I mean?"

The dogs went down on all fours again and nodded their heads, as if to say, *Yes, we know just what you mean.* Sullivan laughed along with everyone else.

"No, no, please don't laugh. It only encourages them. Let's see if I can teach them to do a basic trick. First, I'll show them how it's done."

The boy got down on his hands and knees. He said, "Paw, Snit!" He held up one hand to show the dog what he meant.

Snit scratched his foot on the ground like a bull. Then he took off and jumped onto the boy's back. He stood on him like a billy goat on a hill. Everyone clapped.

"Please don't clap!" said the boy. "You can see what bad dogs they are."

Now the other one, Snoot, came forward. He hunched down and squeezed under the boy as if he were a bridge. And stayed there.

The woman in black began to play "For He's a Jolly Good Fellow."

"No, no! No music!" the boy pleaded.

The music ground to a halt. Snoot came out from under the boy and began to lavishly lick his face.

"Ugh! Stop kissing me! And Snit, you get off!" The boy struggled to his feet, pushing the dogs away. He stepped forward to the edge of the stage and held out his hands in a gesture of wanting sympathy.

"Ladies and gentlemen, I apologize for this terrible

act. I really expected things to go better today. I can only hope that you enjoy the other acts more than this one . . ."

While he talked, Snoot left the stage and came back pushing a large red ball. Behind the boy's back, he rolled the ball to Snit. Snit tossed it up in the air with his nose and Snoot knocked it back. Snit stopped the ball, jumped on top of it, and moved his feet so that the ball rolled across the stage with him on top while Snoot ran circles around it.

"What are you laughing at?" asked the boy. "I'm trying to apologize. I'm being serious here." People shouted at him to turn around. "What's that? Turn where?" Finally, he did, and saw what the dogs were up to. "You bad dogs!" he shouted, and chased them off the stage. The curtain closed, music struck up, and everyone clapped. Jinny and Sullivan clapped, too.

Master Melville bounded forward. "That poor boy doesn't look very happy about his dogs, does he? But I can tell you, one sip of Master Melville's Hop-Hop Drops will make the world of difference for him after the show. Because, yes sir, they're absolutely safe for children. No doubt some of you out there feel that life could be a little better. A little happier. Some of you no doubt suffer from anxiety, depression, fears, dyspepsia, bad moods, no zip, flatulence, or just general grumpiness. Then these drops will help you. And they are available exclusively from yours truly — for a mere ten dollars a bottle. But first, we have one more act to lighten your heart, for it is our desire to bring you happiness in all its manifestations. And after that, Mistress Melville and I will be glad to part with some of our precious supply of drops. Please remember, no pushing, and there is a limit of five bottles per person. But now, let me present to you another young performer, a true artist in her chosen calling, the Angel of the Air, *Miss Esmeralda!*"

Master Melville stepped aside. The audience grew quiet. The music began, a single scratchy note, and Sullivan saw that Mistress Melville had hung the banjo-ukulele on a hook at her waist and had taken up in its place a violin. She began to play something classical (not very well, Sullivan thought), and he turned his gaze back to the stage as the curtain opened. A rope had been suspended across it, perhaps three feet off the ground and sagging slightly in the center. The violin began to play faster, if no less scratchily. From one side of the stage, a bare pointed foot appeared. The foot glided forward along the rope, attached to a slim leg clad in pink tights. Then a ruffled skirt or tutu of a peculiarly bright orange appeared, followed by a small, limp hand and a thin wrist, then a leotard top of black and yellow polka dots, and finally the rest of the girl with the red hair—the same girl who had appeared outside the magician's haunted house the night before. She had pale skin and long, almost white eyelashes and countless freckles.

The girl walked slowly, almost effortlessly, to the middle of the tightrope, wobbling only a little. At the center she raised one foot, brought her arm down, and then she was standing on her hands, legs straight up in the air. She did a couple scissor kicks before coming back to her feet as the audience clapped.

After that the girl struck a series of ballet-like poses, holding each for several seconds before moving again. She then *ran* along the rope, back and forth, fluttering her arms rather like, Sullivan had to admit, a chicken trying to get away from the farmer's ax. And then she did something quite extraordinary; not exactly artistic, maybe, but certainly unusual. She lay on the rope, hands clasping it at one end and ankles at the other, and then in this horizontal position proceeded to spin around it, like a bead turning on a string. She went faster and faster, and the music became more and more frantic, until she flung herself up into the air and then landed in a split.

There was a great roar of approval from the crowd,

and much whistling and stamping of feet. "She's splenderful," said Jinny.

Sullivan thought that Jinny was right. The girl was "splenderful," in just about every way. He watched as she curtsied, smiled, and ran off the stage. The curtain closed.

"This humble show of ours," said Master Melville, reappearing once more, "is presented free of charge, gratis, with our compliments. If it has lightened your evening a little, filled your inner vessel with a cup or two of joy, then we have succeeded in our self-appointed task. And I want you to know without equivocation that I don't want you to even consider buying a bottle of Master Melville's Hop-Hop Drops if you never feel down in the dumps, out of sorts, or just plain sad. If you are one of the lucky few, one of the truly happy people of this world, then my drops can do nothing for you. But for all others, take note that we will be selling bottles at the side of the stage. There will be no need to push or jostle, we have enough for everyone. I shall dispense the bottles while my better half, the companion of my life and one of the great beauties of our time, Mistress Eudora Melville, will handle all financial transactions. I do not know when next we shall grace your fair village, as our work takes us to the most far-flung destinations. But until we meet again, may I say good luck, good health, and great happiness!"

Master Melville made a very deep bow. People were already stepping past Sullivan to get to the side of the caravan. He took Jinny's hand and the two of them watched as Mistress Melville, who had taken off her musical suit of armor, now placed herself at a small table with a little metal money box on it. "Is she a princess?" Jinny asked. "Or maybe she's a witch. Do you think those drops would make Mom and Dad happy? They seem awfully worn out."

"I don't know," Sullivan said, although he'd been wondering the same thing. "Anyway, we don't have ten dollars."

Jinny sighed. "One day," she said, "I'm going to have a machine that makes ten dollars whenever I want it."

"That's counterfeiting."

"It is? Now I know what I want to do when I grow up. I want to be a counterfeiter."

But plenty of other people had lined up and were handing the woman ten- and twenty-dollar bills. Her blood-red lips never smiled or spared a word. Next to her, Master Melville pulled the little glass bottles from a wooden crate and handed them over with a word, a grin, a handshake.

"Let's go home," Jinny said, looking up at the sky.

Sullivan, too, saw how the evening had turned. Distant trees and fences had become black silhouettes. But Sullivan didn't want to go yet. He felt held there as if by a strange power, a magnetic force almost. "We'll be just another minute," he said.

He joined the line, Jinny sulking beside him. Each time the woman at the table took a bill, she held it to the light of the lantern before putting it in the metal box. Each time Master Melville handed out a bottle, he said, "Yes, immediate results, you'll see," or "Not more than a sip now, it's formulated for maximum potency!"

At last Sullivan and Jinny reached the front of the line. Mistress Melville licked her finger — she had long pointed nails, painted black — and rifled through a pile of bills. She looked at Sullivan with unblinking dark eyes, making him blush.

"A young customer, I see," said Master Melville, patting Sullivan on the shoulder. "And how many bottles would you like?"

"I'm sorry. I don't have any money."

"No money? This is not a charity, young man. There are real customers waiting. Get along with you."

"Give the boy a moment," said the woman.

Master Melville glanced at his wife. "A moment? Certainly, my dear." And he looked back at Sullivan.

"I can . . . I can juggle," Sullivan stuttered.

"But you never show anyone," Jinny whispered.

"Can you, now?" said Master Melville. "How delightful. Perhaps you also make bird sounds and do yo-yo tricks."

But Sullivan was not deterred. From the pocket on one side of his jacket he brought out two balls. From the pocket on the other side he brought out two more.

"You're a bit young to juggle four balls, don't you think?" Master Melville said, not unkindly. "I salute your ambition, I really do, but I have sales to make —"

What Sullivan did next was so totally unlike him that he hardly felt he knew himself at that moment. He began to juggle. He tossed the balls up in succession and began a shower pattern, throwing a little higher each time. He had never successfully done a full 360-degree spin with four balls. What's more, he was standing on uneven ground and it was too dark to see well. But he tried it now, turning on his heel so fast he felt dizzy, returning just in time to catch and toss the balls again.

"Wow!" gasped Jinny.

One . . . two . . . three . . . four — he caught the balls and stashed them back into his pockets.

Master Melville frowned as he watched. But then he broke into a smile. "Well, well! I didn't expect that. A talented boy. Don't you agree, Eudora?"

The woman, too, was studying him. What he had just done began to sink in, and Sullivan felt so faint that he thought he might keel over. Mistress Melville looked him up and down as if he were something for sale in a shop window.

"Some little talent," she said at last. "But see how pale he's gone."

"Young man," said Master Melville, clasping Sullivan's shoulder with his hand. "Do me the favor of returning tomorrow evening. We don't usually stay three nights, but we can make an exception. I have something for you. Something that will be of great use to you."

Sullivan, finding himself unable to speak, nodded. Then he took Jinny's hand and they turned around and began to hurry home.

❄

Fortunately for Sullivan, his parents had been too busy dealing with a minor crisis at the Stardust Home to realize that he and Jinny had gone out. One of the residents, Thackery Muldoon, had a pet mouse, which had escaped and slipped under Emily Potterfield's door. There had been a great deal of screaming, and the mouse had almost been flattened by a silver tea tray before Sullivan's father had managed to rescue it. By the time everyone was settled down again, Sullivan and Jinny were at home in their pajamas.

Sullivan got Jinny into bed, a nightlight glowing in the corner, and sat down beside her.

"Sullivan," she said, turning under the covers, "why can't I tell Mom and Dad about the medicine show?"

"Because . . . because I want to surprise them with a bottle of Hop-Hop Drops. That's why I'm going to go back tomorrow, to buy it. So you can't tell them about that, either."

"Okay."

"You pinky swear?" Sullivan held out his finger.

"I pinky swear," she said, hooking her little finger around his.

Sullivan went back to his own room. In truth, he wasn't sure why he had asked Jinny to keep the medicine show a secret. Maybe it was because he didn't think his parents would let him go back again tomorrow if he told them about it. Maybe it was because he didn't know what Master Melville wanted to show him. Sullivan couldn't imagine what it might be, but he had a feeling it was something great and important, something that might even change his life.

He tried to read for a while, but he couldn't concentrate, so he went to say good night to his parents.

They were back in the upstairs sitting room, just as they'd been when he had last seen them. While his father worked at his knitting, his mother read aloud a new poem that she had written.

In all the world, the thing I hate
Is when I find only one ice skate.
Or my kite has got stuck up in a tree
Or my book has no page fifty-three.

I like to finish what I start
Whether it's playing a tune or cooking a tart.
But a guitar's no good with a broken string
And a tart's no tart if it's got no filling.

The answer, I guess, is to take more care
Of the things I play, and make, and wear.
But it's not my fault, you can't blame me
If my book has no page fifty-three.

"That's absolutely gorgeous, my dear," said Sullivan's dad. "I think that's your best poem in the last two weeks."

"Do you really?" said his mom. "I'm not so sure about the 'filling' line. It doesn't scan very well."

"You are too much the perfectionist, Loretta."

Sullivan said, "I've just come to say good night."

"Did you lay out the dishes for the morning?" asked his dad.

"I never forget, do I?" Sullivan hadn't meant it to sound angry.

"That's true. I'm sorry."

"Are you all right?" asked his mom, getting up. "I know we ask a lot of you. Do you want me to come and sit with you for a bit?"

"No, that's okay."

"Is something else bothering you, Sullivan?"

Sullivan hesitated. *Was* something bothering him? Not telling his parents where they had gone tonight — that bothered him. Samuel Patinsky's taunts — that bothered him, too. That it was okay for his mom to write poetry and his dad to always want to run his own business but not for them to take his juggling seriously — that definitely bothered him. That he was planning to lie to them tomorrow night, too . . .

"No," he said at last. "Nothing's bothering me." And he went back to bed.

THE SOFT CLICK

HE kids of Beanfield Middle School thought that their school was better than the ones in nearby Pittsville, Greenhaven, and Halliwell. And they liked to tell each other why.

"Our gym doesn't smell as bad as Pittsville's."

"The kids at Greenhaven wear the ugliest shoes in the world."

"At Halliwell the science teacher is missing a finger."

Unlike most of the other kids, Sullivan had actually been to other schools. He knew that the Pittsville gym didn't smell any worse than theirs and that the kids at Greenhaven wore the same shoes as everyone else. It *was* true that the Halliwell science teacher was missing his finger—Sullivan had gone to Halliwell. Sometimes he told the kids that he lost it to a tiger at the zoo, sometimes that he suffered frostbite while climbing Mount Kilimanjaro, and sometimes that he had simply forgotten where he put it. Actually, he was a pretty good teacher.

Sullivan was having these thoughts when he should have been concentrating on the dodgeball game they were playing in gym class. Which was why it was so easy for Samuel Patinsky to nail him with a terrifically hard shot. The ball smacked into Sullivan's stomach, and he yelped as he crumpled to the floor.

"Hey, Mintz," Samuel called out. "Try not to make it so easy for me. It just isn't as satisfying."

"That throw was overhand," said Norval, helping Sullivan up. "It should be disqualified."

"That's my call," said Mr. Luria, the gym teacher. "And I say it was a fair throw." Sullivan thought that Mr. Luria must have once been the Samuel Patinsky of *his* school.

"You going to be okay?" Norval said to Sullivan.

"I . . . think . . . so," Sullivan gasped. "Soon as . . . I can . . . breathe again."

The rest of the day did not go much better. It didn't help that all Sullivan could think about was going to see the medicine show that night. During math, when the teacher asked him to go up to the board, he had no idea what the question was. At lunchtime, he dropped half of his sandwich (leftover pancakes between two pieces of bread) on the floor and spilled his juice. And he tried to hide behind a book when, for English, his teacher wrote one of his mom's poems from the newspaper on the board and asked them to write a paragraph analyzing it.

I wish that I was two feet taller
And my eyes were sparkling blue.
I wish I could win a Nobel Prize
For inventing a kind of glue.

I wish I played in a punk rock band
And was friends with a movie star.
I wish that I could wave my hand
And bring an end to war.

But if I don't win a prize one day
Or travel the world so far,
I guess it'll really be okay —
As long as I'm friends with a movie star.

Maybe the teacher thought he was being nice to Sullivan, but the truth was that Sullivan felt only mortification. He didn't like how nobody ever noticed him in school, but that didn't mean he wanted to be known as the son of the Bard of Beanfield. He didn't want to analyze his own mother's poem either; it felt icky, like having to watch your parents dance at a wedding. And when he looked up from his paper, he saw Samuel Patinsky shooting him resentful glances, as if the assignment was Sullivan's fault.

At last, the final bell of the day rang and Sullivan rushed down to the first floor. At the door of the grade one class he met Jinny's teacher, a hugely tall woman with frizzy hair named Ms. Compton. "You're such a good big brother, taking care of your sister," Ms. Compton said. Sullivan took Jinny's hand, and as soon as they were outside he started to run.

"Hey," Jinny protested. "You're going to pull my arm off!"

"Okay, okay, but hurry up."

"It's such a nice day, I think I'll walk slow."

"I hate you!" Sullivan growled.

"I'm going to tell Mom and Dad you hate me."

"Go ahead. Tell the world for all I care."

"Anyway, I hate you worstest."

At home, Sullivan rushed through his chores and

then went up to his room to get his homework more or less done. He took his juggling equipment out of the drawer and laid it on his bed — his two sets of balls, his rings, and his clubs. He had already decided that he would bring them all in case Master Melville asked to see his juggling again. The very thought made him tremble, but he was determined not to freeze up. Master Melville was in show business. He could give Sullivan all kinds of tips and hints for performing better. And maybe, well, just maybe . . . Sullivan's face grew hot.

For the truth was that Sullivan had spent half of last night in a glorious fantasy. He imagined Master Melville, standing in front of the curtains, saying, "Ladies and gentlemen, tonight there is a special person in the crowd. A young person of amazing ability. And if we applaud very loudly perhaps we can convince him to come up and show us his juggling skills. Ladies and gentlemen, I give you . . . *Sullivan!*" And Sullivan would climb onto the stage without the slightest fear and juggle better than he had ever juggled in his life.

All right, he knew that wasn't going to actually happen. Still, he wanted to be prepared for whatever opportunity might arise, which meant that he had to practice. So he picked up three balls, got in his proper stance, began to throw . . . and dropped the balls.

"No, no, no!" Sullivan growled at himself. He picked them up and tried again. He managed five throws before tossing one so wildly that he had to lunge for it, causing him to miss his next throw. *Calm down, calm down!* he told himself. And slowly he did, even if he still made mistakes. He practiced with three balls, then four (hopeless), then rings. It was when he picked up his clubs that he heard a voice at his door.

"Looks like you're having quite a workout."

It was Manny Morgenstern. Somehow Manny always knew when Sullivan was practicing. He had already decided not to tell anyone about the medicine show, not even Manny, although he still hadn't been able to come up with a very clear reason why. Perhaps he simply wanted to keep what he knew, at least for a little while, just for himself.

"You know, just staying out of trouble," Sullivan said, using one of Manny's expressions.

"That's what I used to say whenever I was getting *into* trouble."

"Manny, was there something you really wanted to do when you were a kid? Something that your parents maybe didn't take seriously? That made you really frustrated because you felt they didn't understand you or really even notice you? So that maybe you felt like you were going to explode?"

"Well," Manny said. "I had this idea of becoming a frog farmer."

"Because," Sullivan went on, "I really want——"

But Manny, thinking back to his own childhood, kept talking. "You see, I had this idea of raising frogs in the backyard. In buckets. I figured that I could raise about a thousand frogs a month. Of course I hadn't quite figured out what to do with them all."

Just then the dinner bell rang. "As soon as I hear that bell my mouth starts to water," Manny said. "I hear your father made lasagna tonight. He does make a swell lasagna."

Much later, Manny would remember this conversation with considerable pain. He would hear again Sullivan's words and realize too late that the boy had needed to talk. If only he had listened properly, Manny thought, he might have heard what Sullivan was really thinking that day. And he might have been able to offer Sullivan a few words of wisdom that would have changed everything.

❄

As always, Sullivan helped serve dinner. He didn't like how quiet it was in the dining room today, the old people concentrating on their food. It was like a restaurant in a silent movie. So he chatted with Mrs. Demopoulos, who showed him a new batch of photographs of her latest grandchild. He let Mr. Orne complain to him about Richard Nixon, even though Richard Nixon hadn't been president for about a million years. When everyone was served, Sullivan sat with Jinny and his parents at their own table.

"And how was everybody's day?" his dad asked.

"Mine was *super* good," said Jinny. "You know what I did all day? I walked on a piperope. On my tippy-toes."

"You mean a *tightrope*," said Sullivan, glaring at his sister.

"Why are you looking at me like that? I didn't say anything about you-know-what."

"What about you-know-what?" asked his mom.

"Oh, that," said Sullivan. "Just Jinny and me playing, that's all."

"I think it's very nice of you to play with your younger sister."

"And it's nice of me to play with my older brother, isn't it?" Jinny said.

"It certainly is," his dad agreed.

"By the way," Sullivan said. "I'm going out for a bit after dinner."

"Out? Where?" asked his dad.

"To a friend's house."

"What friend?"

"Norval. We have a school project to do."

"I'm glad to see you going to another boy's house. What's the project on?"

Sullivan hesitated—he hadn't thought that far ahead. But Jinny blurted out, "Bananas! His project is on bananas."

"Bananas?" asked his dad.

"Sure," Sullivan said. "They're a pretty interesting fruit, when you really think about them."

"I'm sure that's very true," said his dad. "And you're just the person to peel back the skin and get to the truth about them. Get it? *Peel?*"

"I got it, Dad."

"Just make sure you don't *slip up.*"

"Okay, Dad."

"And no *monkeying around* at Norval's. As soon as you're done, you better *banana split* right out of there."

Sullivan's mom patted his dad on the hand. "Just stop it, dear."

❊

There are moments in life when, even as you are determined to do something, you know that it is wrong. You may not know why and so you dismiss the feeling as cowardice or laziness or some other personal failing, rather than for what it is—a warning from some deep part of the brain.

That was what Sullivan felt, packing his juggling

equipment into his backpack. It was an unpleasant, almost sick feeling, but he pushed it back down from wherever it came, went to the front hall, put on his jacket, and headed out. Walking alone, he regretted not having found a way to take Jinny with him. The streets felt very empty and the light was already dimming. He got to the corner where he would have turned for Norval's house, hesitated, and kept going. He walked faster and faster until finally he broke into a run. He went past the store, and then the first farm, to Reingold's Field. Approaching the stand of trees, he could see that the show had already started.

Sullivan joined the audience at the back and saw that the arrogant young magician was performing. He edged up through the crowd and managed to get to the front but was pushed to one side by some teenage boys. The magician had laid a wooden board over two sawhorses and was now helping the girl with red hair lie down on it. He passed his hand over her face and her eyes closed, as if she had fallen asleep. He covered her with a sheet and then, very slowly, pulled one of the sawhorses out from under the board. Even though the girl was now supported at only one end, she didn't fall.

Slowly he pulled away the other sawhorse. The board with the red-haired girl on it remained in the air, floating. Sullivan thought he knew how the trick was done, but when the magician moved a hoop so that she passed through it, his theory was pretty much shot.

The crowd clapped and the magician put the saw-horses back, pulled off the sheet, and woke the girl before helping her down.

Master Melville came out and talked about Hop-Hop Drops. He used almost exactly the same words as yesterday, only this time he looked over at Sullivan and winked. Sullivan smiled. He felt rather important, being recognized by Master Melville, as if he wasn't a regular part of the audience but someone on the "in-side." Next, the automaton Napoleon was brought out and a woman in office clothes volunteered. The game took longer than the night before, but the woman lost.

The two small dogs, Snit and Snoot, took the stage with the small boy. Sullivan realized with a shock that the whole performance was an act. The dogs disobeyed the boy because they were supposed to. In fact, Sulli-van could see that by using little hand movements and nods, the boy was actually signaling to them. Every so often he slipped them a little treat as a reward. But it was all done so cleverly that Sullivan admired the act even more.

The last to come on was the girl with red hair. This time he saw something in her face that he hadn't seen before, a quiet sadness. But what could she be sad about, he wondered, when she got to perform on a real stage? He wondered if it was part of her act, like the boy's bumbling.

And then she looked at him.

The girl was just about to jump off the end of her tightrope when she stared directly at him. Not for a fleeting moment, but for several seconds. She couldn't have been looking at anyone else, he was sure of it. Her eyes were clear, and slowly she shook her head. Just a little. Did she mean "no"? Did she mean "don't"? The curtain closed. He was flattered that she would notice him, and pushed away the unsettling feeling that her expression had given him.

"Ladies and gentlemen," called Master Melville, stepping out in front again. "Usually this is the end of our entertainment. But tonight we have a special treat for you, something rarely presented due to its tremendous degree of difficulty. A magical illusion called *The Vanishing Box*. I will ask our brilliant young magician, the Great Frederick, back onto our stage."

The curtains drew back and the magician wheeled out a large, rectangular wooden box about the size of a small coffin. He turned it in a circle, knocking hard on each side. He opened the lid and tipped it to show the bottom. Then he put the lid down again.

"I need a volunteer," said the magician. "That is, if anyone is brave enough. One person willing to have the molecules of his body dissolved to their individual parts so that they might travel through space and reassemble elsewhere. I can promise you that not one hair on your head will go missing. Of course, I can't guarantee that you will be reassembled in exactly the right order."

The magician gave an artificial laugh. He gestured out to the audience. "Do we have a volunteer?"

Three or four kids in the audience, boys and girls both, eagerly put up their hands. A couple of them even called out, "Pick me!" Sullivan watched curiously, interested to see if it mattered to the magician which volunteer he actually chose. Most likely, he would select somebody who was the right size to make the trick work, or someone who looked cooperative. Frowning, the magician held his hand to his brow and scanned the crowd from one end to another. His face changed, as if recognizing the perfect volunteer, and then he pointed his finger directly at . . . Sullivan.

"You! Yes, you. Thank you for volunteering. If you would just come up onto the stage."

Sullivan hadn't even put his hand up, but he did as he was told. Perhaps the magician preferred someone who wasn't eager. Or perhaps Master Melville had

singled him out as a fellow performer of sorts, someone who wouldn't give away any secrets.

The Great Frederick didn't hold out his hand, so
Sullivan had to climb up himself. Without asking, the
magician pulled Sullivan's backpack off and tossed it
to the side. It was Sullivan's first time on a stage, and
even though he didn't have to perform, he still felt his
stomach somersault. The light of the kerosene lamps
in his eyes turned the audience into nothing more than
dark forms beyond the first few upturned faces. He
realized with disappointment that the magician had
likely pointed to him merely by chance.

Frederick opened the lid of the box. Mistress
Melville began to play eerie music on a little accor-
dion. "Look inside," Frederick commanded. "Tell the
audience what you see."

Sullivan looked inside. He saw a sheet of paper
with words on it:

Say, "I can see the moon and the stars.
I can see the whole universe."

Sullivan obeyed the instruction. "I can, ah, see the
moon and the stars. I can see the whole universe."

The magician said, "Please, step into the box. Step
into the universe and join the moon and the stars."

Sullivan did as he was told. He stepped in with one foot and then the other. He felt the magician's hand on his shoulder begin to push him downward. Sullivan went along, bending at the knees, then leaning forward and putting his hands onto the bottom of the box.

"And where will the boy next appear?" said the magician. "London? New York? Ancient Rome? Or perhaps the future. That, I cannot predict . . ." As he spoke, he slowly closed the lid of the box. The light began to disappear and then, with a thud, the lid was down and Sullivan was in pitch darkness.

He remained uncomfortably on his hands and knees. The darkness was a little freaky. He couldn't hear anything, either — the box muffled sound. He wondered what the magician was saying. He wondered what he, Sullivan, was supposed to *do*. Would a mirror make it look as if he were no longer in the box when he really was?

And then he heard a soft click. There was something about the sound of that click that made his heart flutter. He felt a jolt, the bottom of the box tilted, and he was sliding down. He tried to grab hold of something, to stop himself, but there was nothing to hold on to.

SPOONITCH AND FORKA

PARENTS have what might be called an internal alarm system. When a parent hasn't seen a child for a certain length of time, depending on where that child is supposed to be, an alarm begins to sound. It starts quietly but quicky grows louder until it can't be ignored.

Loretta Mintz was taking a load of sheets out of the dryer in the basement when she realized she hadn't seen Sullivan return from Norval's house. Mind you, she knew that son of hers could lose track of time worse than his father. She was glad he had gone to

Norval's and hoped that he was having such a good time he didn't want to come home yet. Sullivan didn't spend enough time with friends — didn't have enough friends, period. Of course, he had a lot of responsibilities, more than most kids. And having moved so much hadn't helped. Loretta felt guilty about both those things. But she also knew that Sullivan was shy and sometimes had trouble getting up the nerve to talk to other kids. He was definitely like her, not like his father, who would make friends with a chicken thief given half a chance.

She came upstairs to find Mrs. Breeze wandering down the hall in her nightgown, calling, "Ginger, come here, Ginger." Ginger was the name of her cat, who had died of old age last year. Sometimes Mrs. Breeze forgot that Ginger was gone. Maybe, Loretta thought, she didn't really want to believe it. She took Mrs. Breeze by the arm and told her that she would ask that nice man who brought his cat to visit the residents to come back again.

Up on the third floor, Jinny was already tucked in bed and Gilbert was reading to her.

"And then Red Riding Hood decided she wanted to become a professional forklift driver."

"It doesn't say that!" Jinny said. "You're making it up."

"I'm not. And look, the Big Bad Wolf wants to buy a guitar and howl his songs in coffeehouses."

"Gilbert," said Loretta. "Sullivan hasn't come home yet."

"Are you sure?" he asked, his eyes still on the book.

"I've looked through the whole house."

"I suppose we should call Norval. It's too dark now for Sullivan to walk home. I'll have to pick him up."

The telephone was in the sitting room. Jinny followed her parents, her blanket wrapped around her and dragging behind. Loretta watched as Gilbert looked through the phone book and then waited for someone to pick up.

"Hello, Mr. Simick? It's Gilbert Mintz. Sullivan's father. Can I talk to Sullivan, please? What's that? No, he told us that he and Norval had a project. Yes, would you mind? Thanks a lot."

Gilbert put his hand over the receiver. "There's a fellow who doesn't know what's going on in his own house. He thinks Sullivan wasn't over tonight."

Loretta felt a little jump in her heart. She panicked easily about her children, and now she waited anxiously for Norval's father to come back on the line. Gilbert began speaking again.

"Yes? Are you sure that's what Norval said? Well, maybe he's not quite telling the truth . . . No, I'm not suggesting that your son is a liar. It's just that . . . All right. Well, thank you."

Loretta stepped toward him. "What is it?" she said.

"Norval says that Sullivan was never there."

"But then where did he go?"

At that moment both parents turned toward their daughter.

"Jinny?" said Loretta.

"Yes?"

"Do you know where Sullivan went?"

"He didn't tell me anything," Jinny said, and started to cry. Her parents thought she was crying because she was worrying about her brother. But actually Jinny was crying because she was telling a lie. She did know where Sullivan had gone. But Sullivan always complained that she told on him whenever he spilled something or didn't finish his homework. So she wasn't going to tell on him now. And as soon as he came home, she was going to let him know what a great sister she was.

"That's okay, sweetie," Loretta said, putting her arm around Jinny. "We'll find your brother."

"Let's phone his other friends," said Gilbert.

"Who?" asked Loretta. "He doesn't have any other friends."

"I'm sure he'll be back any minute. He probably took a walk. Maybe he met a girl he likes."

"Gilbert, he's too young."

"Of course he's not too young. When I was his age I fell madly in love with Melissa Frimp. She had a gap between her two front teeth. I thought it was adorable."

"This isn't the time, Gilbert. We need to find Sullivan."

"All right. I'll drive around the neighborhood. I'll check the school and the park. You phone every person we know. He'll show up."

The Mintzes didn't own a car, so Gilbert went next door and borrowed the neighbors', after they made him promise to be careful not to scratch it. He drove slowly up and down the streets with the windows open, calling out, *"Sullivan! Sullivan! Are you there?"* He pulled up by the school and walked to the middle of the field. He called again. He did the same at the park and in the parking lot of the supermarket. He asked a man walking his dog if he had seen a boy. He asked a woman getting out of a taxi. When he saw a pay phone, he stopped to call home.

"Hello?" Loretta said. "Sullivan?"

"No, it's me. There's no sign of him."

"I'm calling the police."

"Right. I'll drive straight home."

In all this rushing about, Jinny's parents forgot to put her to bed. She waited for the police to arrive, her blanket still wrapped around her. Manny Morgenstern had come upstairs to wait, too. He had been having trouble sleeping and heard their footsteps overhead. When the doorbell rang, Gilbert hurried down and then ushered two police officers in uniform into the sitting room.

The man was short, stout, balding, and had a little mustache. "I'm Officer Spoonitch," he said.

"And I'm Officer Forka," said the woman, who was tall and skinny and had large teeth.

"You're kidding," said Gilbert. "Spoonitch and Forka?"

"Please, no jokes," said the woman officer. "We've heard them all."

"Of course not," Loretta said. "This is a serious matter. Our son is missing."

"Surely not missing, ma'am," said Officer Spoonitch. "Just late. Happens all the time. Has he ever run away?"

"Never," Gilbert said. "And our son is never late. We don't even know where he's gone."

"If I might say something," offered Manny Morgenstern.

"Are you a relation?" asked Officer Forka.

"No, a family friend. I know this boy, Sullivan, very well. He wouldn't run away. He's very responsible. If he hasn't come home it's because he can't."

"Oh, my!" Loretta gasped.

"I'm sorry, I didn't mean to upset you," Manny said. "But wherever Sullivan is, he needs our help."

As each of the adults spoke in turn, Jinny watched them from behind the sofa. When she was a baby she had sucked her thumb, and although she had stopped more than a year ago, she now put her fist to her face, rubbing the side of her nose with her finger just as she used to. Jinny had listened with increasing alarm and a terrible feeling that somehow Sullivan going missing was all her fault. She had lied and now the police were here and still Sullivan hadn't come home. She wanted to speak, but no words came out of her mouth. Jinny took a deep breath and tried once more, and this time the words poured out so quickly that they tripped over one another.

"Sullivan and I went to see this show, it was about doctors, and it was in the field, and there was a magician who grabbed cards out of the air and this funny kind of robot that played chess and two dogs who were so naughty and a girl on a piperope and this man who sold these drops in little bottles, and then after, Sullivan went up to the man and told him he could juggle and I think he was going back but he didn't actually tell me and also there was this beautiful woman with skin so white and long black hair and she played a big drum and—"

The doorbell rang and everyone jumped up. Jinny stopped talking. "Perhaps I'd better get it," said Officer Spoonitch, and he went downstairs while the rest waited. No one spoke, and finally Officer Spoonitch returned with a very young policeman carrying an ordinary plastic shopping bag. Officer Forka went over and the three whispered together a moment.

"Mr. and Mrs. Mintz, does your son have a green jacket?" asked Officer Forka.

"Yes," said Loretta. "Why do you ask?"

Officer Spoonitch took the plastic bag from the young policeman. From it he carefully pulled a jacket, holding the bag under it, for the jacket was sopping wet.

"Let me see," Gilbert said, hurrying over to take it. "Yes, yes, this is Sullivan's. Does that mean you've found him?"

"No, we only found the jacket," said Officer Forka.

"But where? Where did you find it?" cried Loretta.

"In the river. Caught on a branch that was bent down into the water. I'm afraid it looks bad. It looks very bad."

Sullivan's mother collapsed on the floor. Gilbert's father, standing frozen with the wet jacket in his hands, was too stunned to try to catch her.

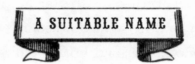

A SUITABLE NAME

DARK.

He felt himself moving. Or inside something that was moving. It rocked and jostled whatever it was he was lying on. Not something hard—not the bottom of the black box anymore. Something soft, if lumpy and uneven.

A bed. He was on a bed, with a thin mattress, a rough blanket, a pillow.

He heard voices. Whisperings. But he couldn't make out any of it.

What had happened? He tried to remember, but his head hurt. The Stardust Home. His mother and father. Jinny. The lid of the wooden box closing.

He lay there, waiting for the dizziness to ease. Slowly he found he could see, if just a little. A crack here and there let gray light into a narrow, shaking room. He began to make out other beds, or bunks, against both walls. And bodies on them. He started to understand some of the whisperings.

"... and I was sure it wouldn't work. The hinge was jammed ..."

"... anything for a nice hot bath ..."

"... well, I feel sorry for him ..."

The last was a girl's voice. Somehow he knew who it was — the girl with the red hair. He felt something rise up his throat, burning. He choked it back down again.

"Why feel sorry for someone that stupid?"

"You were that stupid once too, you know."

"He's no worse off than the rest of us."

"But he's new. It's the hardest period."

"I just hope he's good. That he can pull his weight. I'm tired of filling in the extra time."

"All you think about is yourself."

"Hey, you guys, keep your voices down. You want the Black Death to hear? I'll tell you what I hope. I hope his family comes looking."

"Not a chance. You know old Melville. He's a master at leaving a cold trail. Nobody ever finds us."

The voices stopped. Someone turned in his bed. Sullivan felt woozy again and closed his eyes. He tried to stay awake, but sleep pulled him under.

❋

When he opened his eyes again, the brightness hurt. He saw sky, branches, figures moving—but vaguely and out of focus. It took a few minutes for everything to become clear.

He was lying on the grass, propped up against the trunk of a tree. There were other trees, spaced evenly apart. It looked like an abandoned orchard, the trees grown wild, dried-up apples on the ground. The caravan with the words *Master Melville's Medicine Show* on its side stood in a clearing. Nearby, the gray horse swished its tail and ate from a bucket.

Sullivan smelled something delicious. Eggs. Sausages. His stomach knotted up and he realized that he was ravenously hungry. Blinking, he watched people moving about. Frederick the magician was standing by a camping stove, stirring the eggs in a heavy cast-iron pan. The girl with the red hair was setting dishes on a table set with a cloth, glasses, silverware. The two small dogs were playing tug-of-war with a bone while the boy who performed with them was sitting on an overturned

• 100 •

box, using a small paintbrush to touch up the side of the caravan. They didn't have their costumes on but wore jeans and running shoes. The girl had her hair tied back. The magician wore a Rolling Stones T-shirt. They looked like ordinary kids.

Sullivan pulled himself to his feet. He felt stiff, as if he'd been asleep for ages, but otherwise all right. Frederick glanced over at him and then, flipping something in another pan, said aloud, "The new boy's up."

The door of the caravan opened. Master Melville stepped out, sniffing the air and looking about, as if to judge the quality of the day. It was somehow a bigger shock to see him in regular clothes—an old plaid work shirt, overalls, scuffed shoes. He scratched the back of his head and yawned as he walked to the table. He looked directly at Sullivan and smiled.

"Let's all have some breakfast," he said.

Everyone stopped what they were doing and came to the table. The magician brought the two pans while the girl brought a tin coffeepot. They sat down, Master Melville taking the place at one end. He motioned to Sullivan.

"Come, take your place," he said, not unkindly. Sullivan came over. There were two empty chairs, one on the end and one beside the small boy. He sat beside the boy. He noticed the other kids looking at him, but when he caught their glances, they turned away. Master Melville served everyone generous helpings, including the plate at the empty endseat, and then said, "Wait."

The caravan door opened and the woman came out. Mistress Melville. She was dressed in a shirt and pants but, as on stage, everything was black. Sullivan realized that she was the person they had been whispering about, the one they called the Black Death. Without a glance in his direction, she took her place at the table, picked up her fork, and began to eat.

"Pour me coffee," she said.

"Of course, sunshine of my life, immediately," said Master Melville, jumping up. Hunger almost overwhelmed Sullivan. He took a forkful of eggs. They were the most delicious he had ever tasted.

"It's the braised onions and the hint of Asiago cheese," said Master Melville, as if reading his mind. "The bread is a crusty pumpernickel, and the sausages — well, those you just have to try. My dearest," he said, addressing his wife, "here is the new addition to our little crew."

"I can see that. I'm not an idiot."

"You are the opposite of an idiot, my sugar plum."

"He juggles."

"You spotted him, my darling one. Just by the look in his eye."

"Well, he'd better be good. And more than good. He'd better have an *act*."

"I don't expect he does, dearest. But he will. Trust me, he will."

"And does he have a name?"

It was extremely disconcerting for Sullivan to be listening to this conversation about him as if he were not at the table. Now, at the mention of his name, he began to speak. "My name is—" But Master Melville thrust his hand toward Sullivan's mouth, motioning for him to stop.

"No, no. Not your *old* name. We don't want to hear that. Not now. Not ever. We need a new name for you. A theatrical name. How about Santiago? No, that's no good. Perhaps Mordechai. Or Valentine or Florentino."

"Look at the boy!" Mistress Melville growled. "He can't carry a name like that. Something more suitable for such an ordinary child."

"You're right as always, my dewdrop. What name, then? I know. Dexter."

"Dexter!" Sullivan couldn't help exclaiming. "That's an awful name."

They ignored him. "Yes, it suits him," said Mistress.

"Now let's not talk about it anymore. In fact, let's have silence. I hate mindless chatter during meals."

"And I enjoy a conversation. It is one of the few very small differences between us, my glazed donut. But I obey your wishes. Not another peep!"

Master Melville kept to his word. Neither he nor anyone else spoke again. Sullivan took one more bite and found that his appetite had disappeared. He sat, listening to the others chew their food, to the clatter of forks and knives. He wondered how far they had traveled from Beanfield and what direction they had gone. He wished that he was in the dining room at home, helping to serve the residents. He wished that he was sitting at his own table, with his mother talking about her latest poem and his father making bad jokes and his sister kicking him under the table.

He heard a noise and looked up to see a crow passing overhead. Then he looked at the still leafless trees and the gray sky. And he tried — tried as hard as he could — not to cry.

When breakfast was over, the girl — Esmeralda — and the small boy — Clarence — began to clean up without being told. Sullivan didn't know what to do, so he just stood up and stepped away from the table. He thought about starting to run, in any direction at all, running as fast and as far as he could just to get away from the caravan and these people. But there are many powerful and conflicting forces that prevent a person from taking action. Fear of making the wrong decision. Fear of being lost, alone, cold, hungry. Perhaps Sullivan's parents were, right now, looking for the caravan. If he ran away, he wouldn't be here when they arrived. And so Sullivan, pulled one way and tugged another by his hammering thoughts, did not run.

Mistress Melville said, "Talk to the boy." Then she got up, sniffed loudly, and began walking toward the caravan. Master Melville watched her until she stepped up through the caravan's door and inside.

"She isn't easy," he sighed. "No, I can't say that. But she's worth it. Let me give you a piece of advice, Dexter. It's best to get on her good side. If you're not, life is only going to be a misery. And it shouldn't be that. It should be good—why, it should be more than good, or what's the point of living at all? Shall we go for a little stroll? There are a few things you need to know."

Sullivan fell in step with Master Melville and they walked between the gnarled trees. His voice was quiet and even gentle. "It's a shock, I'm sure, finding yourself here. A terrible shock. You must be very upset. And no doubt thinking of your loved ones back home. But life can be very surprising. And really, we are all on a sort of journey, aren't we? A journey with unexpected twists and turns."

"I have to go home," Sullivan said. "My parents will be frantic. They must be looking all over for me. I lied to them. I need to let them know I'm safe and that I'm coming home or they can pick me up."

"Ah, but that's the thing, dear boy. You can't go back. Not just yet."

Sullivan stopped, and Master Melville did, too. They stood under a tree with branches that looked to Sullivan as if they were reaching down to grab him. "Why can't I go back?"

"For one thing, if we let you go back, the police will think—well, they'll think we tried to kidnap you. Which of course is not the case at all. Your falling through that false bottom—it was an accident, a faulty latch. We had no idea you were still in there. But the police assume that people like us, traveling performers, are thieves and cheats. People of the lowest morals. It's a terrible prejudice. They'd go very hard on us if we took you back now."

"But I'll tell them that you didn't kidnap me. I'll tell them it was like you said—an accident."

"I'm sure you would, dear boy. I've absolutely no doubt of your sincerity. But the authorities aren't very keen on believing children, either. They think little more of them than they do of us. What we need is a little time for the emotions to calm down. That's all."

"If you just let me off somewhere, in some town, I could telephone. I wouldn't tell them anything about you. I'd say that I ran away. And jumped on a train or got a lift with a truck driver."

Master Melville smiled. He patted Sullivan on the shoulder and then left his hand there. "I can see you're clever. And there's nothing more appealing than a clever boy. We're going to get along splendidly. We're going to be real friends. But you see, there is another reason you can't go back. A reason that has nothing to do with us and everything to do with you."

"I don't get it."

Master Melville took a deep breath. "I wish that I didn't have to show you this. I wanted to avoid doing so. It will upset you. But I see that I have no choice."

From the big pocket of his overalls he drew a folded sheet torn from a newspaper. He unfolded it, looked at it a moment, and then reluctantly handed it to Sullivan.

"Here, poor child. Read about your fate."

Sullivan took the paper. Near the bottom, a small article had been circled in black ink.

LOCAL BOY MISSING, BELIEVED DROWNED
Special to the Beanfield Gazette

A tragic event yesterday has left one local family and the residents of a retirement home in grief. Eleven-year-old Sullivan Mintz, son of Gilbert and Loretta Mintz, went out last night and did not return. Shortly after the Mintzes, who operate the Stardust Home for Old People, called the police, the boy's jacket was found floating in the Hasberg River. The police have concluded that the boy drowned while playing on the riverbank. It is believed that the current carried his body into the deepest part of Lake Serenita.

News of the tragedy spread quickly through Beanfield Middle School. "He was like my best friend," said Samuel Patinsky. "I mean, this is going to be hard on me. I might even need to stay home from school."

A memorial service will be held at the Stardust Home tomorrow evening.

"But I'm not dead!" Sullivan cried. "I'm alive! I'm right here! We've got to tell them. My parents and my sister, they'll be so sad. We've got to hurry!"

In his excitement, Sullivan had grabbed hold of Master Melville's sleeve, pulling on him, as if to get him to take Sullivan home right this moment. Master Melville looked down at Sullivan's hand and for a moment his face grew dark. But then he smiled again, gently removing the boy's hand. "Yes, I'm sure this is very hard on them. But you know, they have already begun to get used to it. They are coming to terms with your death."

"But I don't want them to come to terms with it! I want them to wish I were still alive."

"But there is something else you don't know. Something the newspaper didn't report. Your father had to go to the hospital."

"The hospital? Why?"

"Because he has, well, a weak heart. I suppose he never said anything, not wanting to worry you. But you must have noticed something. Weary sighs. Fatigue."

"I did see him asleep in his chair the other day."

"Exactly," Master Melville said, gravely shaking his head. "Now it's imperative that he be very careful. His recovery depends on it. The shock of losing you was a terrible blow, but finding out that you're actually alive—that could put him over the edge. It could be fatal."

"You mean, if my father found out I was alive, it could kill him?"

"Later, when he's had a full recovery, you can

certainly go back. As long as your parents' other problems are sorted out."

"You mean their financial problems?" Sullivan asked, with increasing despair.

"Yes, their financial problems. That's just what I mean. I expect you have noticed that your parents are always short of money."

"Sure, but that happens to people. They have to be careful about spending."

"That's nothing compared to the crisis your parents are in. To be blunt, they are on the verge of losing everything. The house, the business, even the furniture. They will be on the street with nothing but the clothes they wear. So you see, your disappearance is a lucky break for them. Children are very expensive, you know. They eat a good deal. They need clothes and shoes and books and all sorts of things. Without you there, your parents might just manage to keep going. So your ending up here is rather a blessing. It is saving your family. Of course, it means that Mistress and I will have to take on the expense of clothing and feeding you for a while. And we are not rich people, oh, no. But we are very *giving* people. As you see, we have taken in others. And we won't abandon you."

Master Melville began walking again. Sullivan caught up to him. All this terrible new information was hard to take in. He said, "But it's only for a little while?"

"Just until your father is well and your parents get back on their feet. Then you can go back. And just imagine what a celebration it will be! What happiness for you all! That is something for you to hang on to, dear boy. The expectation of that moment. And in the meantime, Mistress and I will treat you like our very own child. Just as we do for these other poor, wayward children. Now come and walk back with me. I can see you shivering there without a jacket. I'm sure I have one that will fit very nicely. And I'm sure for the show tonight I can find you some small, useful job. You would like that, wouldn't you?"

Sullivan tried to calm his own breathing. He said, "If I'm going to be here, then I'd like to be useful. Like the other kids."

"That's the spirit. I could see just what sort of boy you were the minute I laid eyes on you."

Master Melville put his arm around Sullivan's shoulder. Deeply upset by all he had heard, Sullivan found the press of the man's arm comforting and un-nerving at the same time. Together, they walked to-ward the caravan.

10

MISHAPS REMEMBERED

DESPITE what he had said about finding something useful for Sullivan to do, Master Melville simply left him alone. Everyone else, on the other hand, seemed to have loads to do. And when they didn't, they were quite content to lie on the grass and go to sleep, or climb an apple tree, or brush down the gray horse, or read an old book with the covers torn off.

In the middle of the afternoon, Sullivan watched Frederick lay out his magician's equipment on the ground. He took out a tackle box like the ones used for fishing gear, and when he opened it Sullivan saw that the little drawers were filled with needles and thread, tiny hinges and almost invisibly thin wire, hooks, clips, elastic bands, thimbles, small mirrors, and various glues and adhesive tapes. The magician began to go over all his equipment, touching up scuff marks, replacing bits and pieces. Sullivan watched, admiring the way Frederick wore his hair (long in front so that he had to keep flicking it out of his eyes) and how quick and precise the movements of his narrow fingers were.

At last Frederick looked over his shoulder at Sullivan. "Are you spying on me?"

"No." Sullivan took a step back. "I'm not a spy."

"Well, you look like a spy. What do you want?"

"Nothing, really. I'm just trying to learn whatever I can."

"Not from me you don't."

"I could help."

Frederick stood up. He stepped toward Sullivan, stopping only inches away. He was thin but tall, and Sullivan had to look up. "Nobody touches my gear except for me. Understand? If you go near my things, if I see you even look at them, I'm going to tear your head off. Get it?"

"I didn't mean anything. I was just trying to be nice."

"And what are you, anyway? A kid who does a little juggling? A rank amateur. The Melvilles know I'm what makes this show special. You'd better just watch yourself, ball boy. Stay out of my way."

"Why don't you pick on someone your own size, Freddy?"

Sullivan took a step away from Frederick and turned to see the small boy, Clarence, standing with his hands on his hips. Clarence was even smaller than Sullivan. But Clarence didn't look afraid. He said, "This tough guy act of yours is a real bore, Freddy. Why don't you go fix your hair? So you can pretend you're a rock star and not just a guy who plays with cards."

"Don't call me Freddy, you shrimp. And what business is it of yours anyway? I'm the headline act. You're a mere time-filler."

"Yeah, well, the audiences like me better than you. Besides, if you're the headline, why is it that Essy closes the show?"

Sullivan watched as Frederick's anger grew, his eyes blazing. "You've gone too far, Tiny. I'm going to hang you upside down by your ankles and shake you until your little brain rattles."

He lunged at Clarence. But his hand swiped through empty air, for the boy had already dodged away. "Come on," Clarence called to Sullivan, running around the caravan. Sullivan hurried after him. They stopped as soon as they got to the other side, where the two dogs were lying under a tree.

"Thanks," Sullivan said. "I guess his bark is worse than his bite."

"No, he'll bite, all right. Kick you too, if he gets a chance. He's nasty. We haven't formally met. I'm Clarence."

The boy held out his hand. Sullivan had never shaken another kid's hand before, but he did now. "And I'm Sull—"

"Don't!" Clarence exclaimed, holding up his palm like a stop sign. "The Melvilles might hear you. They have ears like elephants. I know your name—it's Dexter. Do you want to meet my dogs? Come here, you two, and say hello to Dexter."

Immediately the two little dogs bounced up and hurried over to Sullivan. They licked his face, making him laugh as he patted them.

"They're not usually so friendly right off, so they must like you," Clarence said. "Of course, they won't go near Frederick. He once kicked Snoot and made her yelp. How old are you?"

"I'm eleven," Sullivan said. "And you?"

"I'm ten. Had my birthday last week. But I'm small for my age, so I look younger. Monty likes that. It impresses the crowd."

"Monty?"

"Montague Melville. Monty's what Mistress calls him, so we do, too—when they're not around. I've been trying to teach the dogs a new trick. Want to see?"

"Sure."

"Okay, Snit. Okay, Snoot. I'm going out now. Don't be too sad."

As soon as Clarence said the word "sad," the dogs stood up on their hind legs. They faced each other, touched paws, and started dancing in a circle. But then they both lost their balance and fell backwards, twisting their little bodies so as to land on all fours.

Clarence shrugged and gave them each a treat and a scratch behind the ears. "They can't stay up for long enough yet."

"Are they your dogs? I mean, were they yours before you joined the medicine show?"

"Sure. That's why Mistress Melville spotted me. She saw me playing with them and teaching them tricks in my front yard while the caravan was passing by. Then Monty came back and left a handbill in the spokes of my bike. The dogs couldn't do nearly as much as they can now. We were just fooling around."

At any other time, Sullivan would have connected the dots, would have come to some logical conclusions based on what Clarence had told him. If the Melvilles had deliberately sought out Clarence, then surely they had deliberately chosen Sullivan, too. Which meant that Master Melville had lied to him. And if he had lied about that, maybe he had lied about everything else. But Sullivan was too upset and confused, and his thoughts were too jumbled, to make those connections. He still believed that his getting trapped in the false bottom of the box had been an accident. He still believed everything that Master Melville had told him. His father had a weak heart. His parents barely had enough money to feed themselves and Jinny and the residents. Sullivan couldn't go home. Not until his father was better and he could find a way not to be a burden to them.

There was no lunch that afternoon (now Sullivan understood why everyone else had eaten such large portions at breakfast), but at dinnertime the table was set again. It must have been Esmeralda's turn to cook, for she brought out a very large pot of pasta in a red-pepper cream sauce. There was also garlic bread and green beans with almonds glazed with honeyed spices. Sullivan couldn't help comparing the amazing flavors with the soft, tasteless food that his father cooked at the Stardust Home. Eating seemed to put everyone in a good mood. There was also, Sullivan detected, a certain rise of energy in anticipation of the evening's show. The performers and Master Melville began to recall and even laugh at themselves for their various stage mishaps. Once, Esmeralda's rope had not been secured properly at one end and, giving way, had caused her to fall onto her rear. Snit had lifted his leg and peed on the curtain. A stream of hidden cards had fallen out of Frederick's sleeve. And one time, Master Melville had taken a dose of Hop-Hop Drops on the stage only to start sputtering and coughing, his face turning purple.

"Not one sale!" he cried, laughing the loudest of anyone. "I didn't make one sale that night."

Only Mistress Melville didn't laugh, or even smile. When her husband finally stopped chuckling, she said, "Sloppy. All signs of unprofessionalism. And nothing to joke about."

"But they are a wee bit funny, my sweet potato," said Master Melville.

"A sense of humor is one thing, I am glad to say, that I was born without."

No one said a word after that until Master Melville, snapping open his pocket watch, declared that it was time.

The table was quickly cleared, the dishes and pots washed in an old tub, and then the caravan was readied. Sullivan guessed that the chores rotated each night. This evening it was Frederick and Clarence who had the task of washing up, and much as they disliked each other, they were able to work together smoothly, without showing any sign of their feelings. Sullivan watched them fold up all the beds and put away any loose objects. Then certain bolts, clasps, and locks were unfastened, and with a crank they lowered the side of the caravan, which became the floor of the stage. The scenery was rolled down and the curtain put up, Clarence making sure it opened and closed properly. Frederick filled the kerosene lamps and hung them. Two tall painted boards were set up, one at either side of the caravan, to act as "wings," behind which the performers could stay out of sight until their entrances.

After that, each person had to prepare for his or her own act. Sullivan watched as props and effects were checked over and put in place. Costumes were pulled on, makeup applied. Frederick loaded his coat with hidden cards, balls, and silks. Clarence checked his pockets for dog treats. Esmeralda powdered her bare feet so they wouldn't slip on the rope. While Master Melville brushed the lint off his jacket and vest, he performed vocal exercises, making weird sounds and exaggerating his lip and tongue movements: "*Oooh . . . aaah . . . eeee.*" And Mistress Melville, having given her raven hair a hundred strokes, strapped on her washboard and cowbells and hauled her big bass drum onto her back. She put the metal contraption holding the harmonica, kazoo, and whistle around her neck. She hung instruments on her belt. She tuned up her banjo-ukulele.

And then there was Napoleon, the chess-playing automaton. Since it couldn't look itself over, Clarence did, opening and closing the little doors. Just as he was latching the last one, Frederick called out, "I see the first marks!" Sullivan didn't understand what he meant until he stepped away from the wings and gazed out across the darkening orchard. Three figures walked toward them. So a mark was a member of the audience, the word part of the secret language of performers.

Suddenly everyone was hurrying past Sullivan. Master Melville pulled the curtains closed, picked a fallen leaf from the stage, and then bowed to his wife on the ground below. She made three loud thumps on the bass drum and then launched into a quick, jaunty number, strumming the banjo-ukulele and blowing into the kazoo, crashing the cymbal and shaking the tambourine. Sullivan felt a hand grab him and pull him behind a wing. It was Clarence. "You can watch from here," he said.

Those three people became five people and then ten people and then more, until there was a good-size crowd, those near the front sitting on the grass and those behind standing. Sullivan stood in the wing, hoping that he would recognize someone, but there was not one familiar face. So he shifted his attention and, for the first time in his life, saw a show from the perspective of a stagehand rather than the audience.

There is a moment, just before curtain, when a transformation takes place, when players leave behind their ordinary beings and become their larger, dramatic selves. It happens whether the stage is large or small, the audience a handful or in the thousands. It happens whether the actors are famous or unknown. And although he could not have described it in words, Sullivan felt it happen. He even saw it in Master Melville's face just before going on—he became eager, smiling, and confident.

He heard the crowd's expectant whisperings and realized that the people out there had changed somehow, too. And then he felt a sharp elbow in his back. "Get out of my way, ball boy!" Frederick almost knocked him over as he went by, leaping onto the stage.

But even though Frederick was nasty to him, Sullivan couldn't help admiring his skill as a magician. Seeing his act from behind revealed many of the secrets of his tricks. He saw, for example, that the cards Frederick was about to pull from the air were hidden against the back of his hand, the corners clipped between his fingers. But his ability to somehow draw a card to the tips of his fingers with a snap made Sullivan appreciate his talent all the more.

He also discovered the secret of the Haunted House. It was ingeniously simple. As Frederick brought out the cardboard sides of the house, Esmeralda crawled behind them, hidden from the audience and already in her identical ghost sheet. And at the moment that Frederick held up the roof of the house in such a way as to block himself from the audience's view for two or three seconds, he and Esmeralda switched positions. Yet to the awed crowd, it was as if the one had transformed into the other.

As Frederick came off the stage, Sullivan wanted to say something about how good he was. Maybe that would soften his attitude toward Sullivan. But he didn't get a chance because Frederick immediately grabbed the collar of the corduroy jacket that Master Melville had given him, lifting him onto his toes.

"If you ever get in my way again I'll beat you until you cry for your mother, who'll never come."

"I'm . . . I'm sorry."

"My act is perfect every time. Get it? And I won't have some little kid who juggles as a hobby mess it up."

"That's enough, Frederick. Let go of him."

Esmeralda had come up from behind Sullivan and laid her small hands over Frederick's much larger ones. Slowly, he let go. "Now go on, Freddy. You've got other chores to do."

Frederick grumbled, but he did as Esmeralda said, walking out past the wing and to the back of the caravan.

"Are you all right?" she asked Sullivan.

"Oh, sure. It was nothing. I wasn't really scared."

"No, I knew you weren't. It's just, well, not everyone understands Frederick." She straightened Sullivan's collar and smiled. "That looks better. I don't think we've properly met. I'm Esmeralda. But offstage everyone calls me Essy. And you're Dexter. It's hard, getting used to a new name, I know. Can I call you Dex?"

"Sure."

"Good. I'd better hurry and get ready for my own act. See you later, Dex."

Sullivan watched Esmeralda—Essy—run around to the back of the caravan, where she would no doubt go into the little tent that had been set up and change into her leotard and skirt. His gaze lingered a moment longer on where she had been and then he turned around again to watch Clarence with Snit and Snoot. He saw how Clarence slipped them little treats after each trick and how, even when he was pretending to scold them, he would nod or give them a quick pat. When they came off stage, the little dogs both jumped up to say hello to Sullivan.

"If you always feel fully and completely happy, my friends, then you do not need my drops and I will not sell them to you for any amount of money."

As Sullivan listened, something occurred to him, something that seemed so totally obvious now that he thought of it. The entire show — the magic, the dogs, the tightrope, everything — had one purpose only. To sell Master Melville's Hop-Hop Drops. Exactly how the show made people want to buy the drops, Sullivan wasn't sure, but he saw that every act led up to the moment when the Melvilles would go to their little table. It was all for the purpose of getting the people to line up at the table. And the people didn't even seem to realize it.

"Are there any chess players in the audience tonight? You, sir? Yes, I'm sure you're very good. Good enough, no doubt, to win against a pile of nuts and bolts . . ."

For the third time Sullivan watched Napoleon play chess, and for the third time he saw its human opponent go down in defeat. It took Napoleon only twelve moves, so fast that the audience didn't have a chance to become deeply involved in the progress of the game. The applause was a mere smattering as the curtain closed.

Master Melville, with Frederick's help, wheeled Napoleon off the stage and down a board to the ground. Sullivan felt it was his chance to speak up, if he was ever going to, so he screwed up his courage and said, "Master Melville? You said there was something useful I could do tonight?"

"Yes, yes, of course," Master Melville said, puffing for breath. "In fact, you can wheel this thing behind the stage with Frederick. It's hard on my old back. That would be most useful, Dexter."

"Sure, I'll help," Sullivan said gladly. Master Melville straightened up, wincing, and Sullivan took his place. As soon as he and Frederick began pushing Napoleon over the trampled grass of the orchard, he felt how heavy it was.

"Watch it! You almost ran over my foot," cried Frederick.

"I'm so sorry."

"You'll be really sorry if you aren't more careful."

They kept pushing until finally they got Napoleon behind the caravan. Frederick stood up and wiped his hands together. "You can take care of the rest," he said, striding away.

"The rest of what?" asked Sullivan, but Frederick was gone. As he stood there wondering what he was supposed to do, he heard a rattling come from inside Napoleon. Surprised, he looked down to see that the entire contraption was shaking.

"Let me out!" came a muffled voice.

"Napoleon?"

"Of course it's not Napoleon! Open the door!"

Sullivan bent down and opened the small front door. "Not that one! In the back!" He fumbled with the latch and got it open, only to see half of Clarence's face! He was breathing quickly, his face red. "There's a button on top. Press it while holding on to its shoulders. Then tilt the whole top backwards. And hurry!"

At first Sullivan couldn't find the button, as it was hidden under a flap of cloth that matched Napoleon's uniform. But finally he pressed it and pushed on the shoulders, and the whole top half of the contraption tilted backwards. He grabbed Clarence's hand and helped pull him out.

"I can't believe it," Sullivan said. "It's a fake! It seemed like a real machine."

"To you and everybody else," Clarence said, stepping out. "Although if you think about it, how could a bunch of cogs and gears be able to see the board, understand the game, and decide on a move? It's pretty silly, really."

"But it doesn't look like a person could fit in there. And I couldn't see you when Master Melville opened the little doors."

"I pull up my knees when one door opens and then lie flat for another. And there are a couple of mirrors, too. Of course, when I started I wasn't much of a chess player. But with all this practice I've gotten pretty good. Being inside there used to be easier, but I've grown. It's hot as anything and I can hardly breathe. Would you mind helping me out next time, too? I hate to rely on Frederick. He pretends to forget and walks away."

"Sure, I'll help. For as long as I'm here, anyway."

"Yes, that's what I mean, of course. Want to go see the rest of the show?"

Clarence and Sullivan went around to watch from the wing, where Master Melville was already standing. He whispered to Clarence, "The game was too quick. Next time you have to string him along."

"I tried. I gave him all kinds of chances. But he was such a bad player, he didn't see them."

On stage, Esmeralda was on the tightrope. Tonight

she did something that Sullivan hadn't seen before —
she stood with two feet on the rope, facing the audience, swung her arms wildly, and somersaulted to
the floor. Now that he had spoken to Essy, it was even
more fun watching her, and he clapped as loudly as
anyone in the audience when she curtsied. When he
looked across to the opposite wing, he saw Frederick
gazing at her adoringly as he clapped, too.

Master Melville made his final pitch, again invit-
ing the audience to buy a bottle of Hop-Hop Drops,
then slipped behind the curtain. Everyone gathered on
the stage, hidden from the crowd, and in their faces
Sullivan saw a glow of energy and pleasure that came
from just having performed. They whispered and joked
and Master Melville praised each of them, which, perhaps despite themselves, made them happy. Sullivan
stayed in the wing, for he knew that he wasn't a part
of this feeling — this relief at the end of the show that
joined them together.

Mistress Melville removed her instruments, and
once more they set up the table next to the caravan.
"Dexter," Master Melville called. "Stand by my side
and hand the bottles to me." Sullivan obeyed, coming up beside them. The bottles were nestled in straw
inside a wooden box, and with each sale he took one
out and handed it to the man or woman. Sullivan had a

chance to examine the bottles as he did so. They were narrow and strangely nice to hold, with slightly long necks and little corks. The labels were cut out with quite elaborate borders, and the words were printed in old-fashioned type. The liquid itself, when Sullivan held it up, was translucent but colored—a vibrant purple if held one way, a deep red if held another.

A man in a cardigan handed over his ten dollars and asked, "What's in those drops, anyway?"

"A proprietary secret, my friend," Master Melville said, handing the money to his wife. "Known only to myself and the great pioneer medicine men of old. And if you want to ask one of them, just go to the third gravestone in the cemetery. He'll tell you before I will!"

When the last bottle was sold and the last audience member had wandered off, the performers had to clean up, for the crowd had left behind food wrappers and plastic bottles and paper cups on the grass. The glow had already begun to fade, leaving behind simple fatigue. And there was something else that Sullivan sensed, almost a feeling of loss, or emptiness. The wings were taken down, as well as the backdrop and curtain and changing tent, and then Frederick turned the crank to pull the stage up while Master Melville hitched up the gray horse. Inside the caravan,

Clarence and Esmeralda set up the four low bunks, which folded down from the walls. Behind the wall opposite the door, Sullivan realized, was a smaller space where the Melvilles must also have had a bed. It wasn't exactly a life of luxury, even for them.

Inside the caravan the children ate a snack of dry biscuits and milk in the glow of a candle, and then Master Melville, knocking on the plywood wall, sent them to bed. They used a basin to wash up and brush their teeth, and they changed into pajamas under their covers. There was a set laid out for Sullivan, just as there had been a toothbrush and a small towel. The pajamas were for a younger kid—they had cowboys and horses on them, and they weren't new. Clarence whispered, "Monty must have snatched them off a clothesline somewhere."

Then there was a sudden jolt, a whinny from the horse, and the caravan began to move. Frederick blew out the candle. No one talked. Sullivan could hear Clarence, who had allergies, wheezing a little. He couldn't sleep. When he closed his eyes he saw his parents' faces, their eyes dark and their cheeks stained with tears. He thought about his father's weak heart and wondered when he might be strong enough again to find out that his son was alive. He thought about their money problems and wished that he could find a way to help rather than be a burden. And when he shook his head to dispel their faces, his sister Jinny's appeared in their place. Poor Jinny—had there ever been a cuter, more lovable sister? Why hadn't he been nicer to her, more kind and helpful? Why had he always been impatient with her? Why did he have to tell her that he hated her, the last time they saw each other? Whenever he got back, he vowed to be the best big brother ever.

He didn't even realize that he was crying. Not until he felt a gentle hand on his arm and heard Esmeralda's voice in his ear. "Shhh, it's okay," she said. "We all feel like that sometimes. Sleep is a real gift for the unhappy, you know. I'll stay right here until you're asleep."

He wanted to tell her that he was glad she was there, but no words came out. Instead, he just closed his eyes.

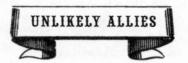

11

UNLIKELY ALLIES

ᴺORVAL Simick had never been to Sullivan Mintz's house or vice versa. They had never hung out at the mall outside of town or become Facebook friends. About the only thing they had done together regularly was have lunch in the school cafeteria.

But when the newspaper published the article stating that Sullivan had drowned, Norval went into his room and refused to go to school. He did go the following day, but he was silent and withdrawn and sad. Mr. and Mrs. Simick knew their son was a sensitive boy, but when a few days later he wasn't any better, they began to consider taking Norval to a doctor.

There is someone else who would have been surprised by Norval's reaction—Sullivan. He didn't believe that he'd made much of an impression on anyone in Beanfield, especially at school. He had no idea that Norval, who had always eaten his lunch alone until Sullivan's arrival, had been grateful for his friendship and had begun to enjoy school more as a result. Norval had seen Sullivan in a way that Sullivan had never seen himself: as smart, sometimes funny, and totally unpretentious.

"This Sullivan must have been a special person," Norval's father said to him. "What was it about Sullivan that you liked so much?"

"He was just a nice guy," Norval answered. "A really nice guy."

The news that Sullivan had drowned—well, that was a genuine blow for Norval. He had experienced one death in his family, his grandfather, when he was a hundred and one. That had been sad too, but the man had experienced a long and full life and, as he'd told Norval on one of his last visits, he felt ready to go. But Sullivan was just a kid. He hadn't really had a chance to do anything yet. He hadn't had a job, or gone to college, or learned to drive, or visited France or China, or had a girlfriend, or performed his juggling for anybody, or done a million other things. It seemed so mean and unfair. And why a nice guy like Sullivan? Why not a stupid bully like Samuel Patinsky?

As it became an accepted fact that Sullivan had drowned, Beanfield Middle School lowered its flag to half-mast. An assembly was called, and all the students shuffled into the auditorium. Beanfield's principal, Mr. Washburb, talked about the importance of safety and the danger of "daredevil activities just to impress your friends," which didn't seem to have anything to do with Sullivan. Pushing his glasses up his nose, the principal said, "I must admit, I don't personally remember Sullivan Mintz. I only know the kids who get sent to the office when they're in trouble. But I've talked to his teachers, and they all liked him. They said he never disrupted class and always got his homework done."

Norval found the assembly highly unsatisfying. There was nothing about the sort of person Sullivan had been. Nobody who actually knew him spoke. And after the assembly, the janitor raised the flag back to the top of the pole.

For the rest of the day, Norval couldn't shake his unsatisfied feeling. He felt so crummy about it that he hardly took in what his teachers said. He wanted to talk to somebody else, somebody who had known

Sullivan, too. But who? It wasn't until near the end of the day that Norval realized something that shocked him. There was only one other person at the school who he was certain had known Sullivan. And that person was Samuel Patinsky.

Samuel had come up to their lunch table almost every day. He had said something mean or sarcastic, and sometimes he had done something mean, too. He'd picked on Sullivan in gym class and had cracked jokes about him in shop. He'd knocked his books out of his hand and tripped him in the hallway. Yes, these were awful things, but at least Samuel had known Sullivan, in a way.

And there was something else that Norval realized. Samuel hadn't been at the assembly. In fact, he hadn't been in school at all that day. Maybe he had a cold. Maybe his parents had taken him on a vacation. Or was there another reason?

Norval just couldn't let go of the thought. He decided that after school he would walk to the Patinsky house and knock on the door.

Samuel Patinsky lived in the opposite direction from the school, at the end of a dead-end road. Norval expected it to be a shabby place, with maybe a broken-down car in the driveway and a mean-looking dog tied on a rope to a tree stump. But instead it was a small yet neat house with a freshly mowed lawn and pink begonias in the planters. Still, it took all Norval's courage to get himself to walk up to the front door, and an extra dose for him not to run away and to ring the bell.

The door opened and a woman that Norval recognized answered. "Mrs P.?" he said in surprise. Mrs. P.—he had never heard her full name—worked as a playground monitor at Beanfield Middle School, making sure kids didn't litter or hurt themselves doing something stupid.

"Why, hello there, Norval. Are you selling popcorn for the Boy Scouts?"

"No, I'm not. Do you live here?"

"For about fifteen years."

"Are you by any chance Samuel's mother?"

"Of course I am. Has Samuel never mentioned it?"

"I guess I forgot," Norval said, although he was sure that Samuel never had. All he ever called her was *the fun police* because she once stopped him from going headfirst down the slide with two little kids that he had forced to sit on top of him. "Is Samuel in?"

"Yes, he's in his room. I hope he hasn't done something to you."

"No, he hasn't."

"Actually, he's been pretty down in the dumps.

What happened to that unfortunate child, Sullivan Mintz, has really upset him. But then, he's a sensitive boy."

"He is?" Norval's voice rose.

"I'm sure it would do him a world of good to see a friend. Come on in."

"I'm not exactly——" Norval started to say, but then he stopped and just followed Mrs. P. through the front vestibule and down a hall. Mrs. P. knocked lightly on a door. "Samaleh? You have a visitor, a friend from school."

Samaleh? Samuel Patinsky actually had a mother who loved him! She opened the door and gently ushered Norval in. Looking around, Norval saw a normal kid's room—model airplanes hanging from the ceiling, piles of comics, an MP3 player on the desk. Even more surprising, Samuel was lying on his bed in bunny-decorated pajamas, with his hands behind his head, staring up at the ceiling.

"Sweetie, it's Norval Simick to see you."

Immediately Samuel sat up with a frown. "Who? Oh, it's you."

"Well, I'll leave you two alone. Norval, see if you can cheer Sammy up."

Norval didn't want Mrs. P. to leave, but she did,

closing the door behind her. As soon as she was gone, Samuel's face took on its usual mean scowl. "Who said you could come to my house?" he said. "I might bash you right now."

"I'll leave," Norval said, reaching for the doorknob.

"No, don't. My mom will just ask me why. You have to stay at least ten minutes. Did some teacher send you because I haven't handed in my homework?"

"Nobody sent me," Norval said. "I just—it's only— oh, it's hard to explain. The truth is, I don't know who else to talk to. You're the only other person who knew Sullivan."

At the sound of Sullivan's name, the most astonishing thing yet happened. Samuel began to cry. It was about the ugliest sight Norval had ever witnessed, and it was painful, too.

"Are you okay?"

"Sullivan . . . is . . . dead. And I was so mean to him."

"If you don't mind my asking, why?"

"I don't know."

"Really?"

"I mean, my big brother was always mean to me. He took my stuff. He called me names. He tripped me and pushed me. Then he went off to college. I thought I'd be glad, and in a way I was, but I was also lonely.

And then I saw this new kid, Sullivan. He looked at me like he was afraid, I guess because I'm kind of big. It made me mad, so I shoved him into a locker. It made me feel like my brother. And it just went on from there. I didn't even enjoy it. And now I wish I'd been his friend. But it's too late."

Norval went over and sat on the bed. Gingerly he reached out, gulped, and put his hand on Samuel's shoulder. He wasn't sure what to say; after all, Samuel really had been mean to Sullivan.

Samuel said, "Did you go to the assembly? I just couldn't. How was it?"

"Honestly? It sucked. Principal Washburb didn't say anything real. Sullivan's going to be forgotten at school in like two seconds."

"But he can't—we can't let him be forgotten!" Samuel said with determination. "Listen to me, Norval—"

"Hey, that's the first time you've ever used my name."

"We can't let Sullivan be forgotten at Beanfield Middle School. I can't take away what I did to him, but at least I can do something. It's up to us to make sure he's remembered."

"Sure, but how?"

"I don't know. Wait, I do know! A day. A special day." Samuel stood up. "You and I have to make, or start, or establish or whatever you call it, a Sullivan Mintz Day. What do you say, Norval? Are you with me on this?"

"Uh, I guess so," Norval said. "Yes. Yes, I'm definitely with you."

"All right!"

Samuel jumped up, and for a moment Norval thought he was going to slug him, but Samuel only patted him on the back.

12

PUNISHMENT

Over the next week, Sullivan learned the routine of Master Melville's Medicine Show. The caravan traveled during the night so that if it passed through any towns or villages it would be less likely to draw attention. Occasionally a person, unable to sleep, might glance out a window, or a worker sweeping the sidewalk or closing up a tavern or baking the next day's bread might look up and see this strange apparition of horse and caravan passing by. But the next day, it would seem like a dream.

Shortly after dawn the caravan would stop by a clump of trees between two fields, or an empty lot—some unattended place not too far from where people clung to the outskirts of a town. Master Melville would rouse the players out of bed, breakfast would be made and served, and then Master Melville and Frederick would take bundles of handbills and set out in opposite directions, placing them at people's doors. The others would work on their routines, or lie under a tree daydreaming, or find another way to pass the time.

Esmeralda had some old schoolbooks—arithmetic, history, science—and she would give lessons to Clarence. And when she was done she would spend time with the gray horse, brushing it, checking its hooves for stones. The Melvilles had no name for it, but the kids called it Soggy, short for Soggy Biscuit, after the famous racehorse named Seabiscuit. The gray was no racehorse, but all of them, even Frederick, liked to pat his nose and talk to him and offer him treats. Esmeralda paid him the most attention, though, and Soggy always raised and then lowered his big head when she came near, wanting her to talk into his ear. The horse tolerated Master Melville, understanding that he was, indeed, his master. He did not like Mistress Melville and whinnied nervously when she came near. But he loved Esmeralda—that, Sullivan could see.

Slowly Sullivan came to believe that Master Melville had lied to him and that he had been deliberately entrapped. He, like the others, was being held against his will. But surely *some* of the things Master Melville had told him were true, and so Sullivan spent his time scheming how to get away when he felt that the time was right—that is, when enough time had passed for his father to recover from the shock of his disappearance and supposed drowning. And also when he had figured out how not to be a financial burden on his parents. But getting away . . . that was the main thing.

First, he considered jumping on the horse and riding off. Only he didn't know how to ride a horse and would probably get thrown and break his neck. Next, he considered sneaking a note to somebody in the crowd that said: *Help! I've been kidnapped! Take me with you!* But wouldn't people think it was part of the act? They might even show it to Master Melville. Or what if they weren't nice people and decided to keep him to plow their fields or wash their floors?

He considered many other plans, too—writing a message on the roof of the caravan that might be seen by a passing airplane, dressing up in some of Esmeralda's clothes and pretending to be a girl. But in the end the one that made the most sense to him was slipping out of the caravan at night. That way the Melvilles wouldn't even know he was gone until morning. The only problem was that Master Melville always locked the back door of the caravan from the outside. With a padlock. A heavy steel padlock.

Sullivan soon realized he couldn't spend the entire day thinking about his escape plan. He had to do something else with his time. The logical thing, he decided, was to practice his juggling. After all, he had brought his equipment in his backpack. (How long ago that seemed! How naive he'd been, expecting to be showered by Master Melville's compliments.)

And so, on the third day of his "captivity," as Sullivan thought of it, he took his backpack from under his bunk in the caravan, found a clear space of grass, and began to juggle. He started with a basic three-ball half-cascade and found himself rusty, or just off somehow, because he kept throwing too high, or too late, or he missed a ball as it came down. One ball even hit him on the head — just as Frederick was walking by with his magician's suit, an ironing board, and one of those old-fashioned irons that you heat over the fire.

"That's a move I've never seen," he said. "Did you invent that all by yourself? What do you call it, the Concussion?"

"I'm a little out of practice."

"Even if you were in practice, you'd stink. But keep it up. I'm sure if you work really hard you'll be merely lousy one day."

And with a snort of laughter he passed by. Sullivan narrowed his eyes at Frederick's receding back. He wanted to say something clever, but all that came out was "Yeah . . . so . . . and you, too." Then he picked up the balls and started again.

After a few minutes his rhythm came back to him. He added the fourth ball—cascade, under the arm, under the leg, spin. He moved on to the rings and the clubs. Juggling is a skill that, like playing a musical instrument or downhill skiing, requires a keen sense of rhythm, an ease of movement, and quick thinking that is both learned and instinctive. It can make a person feel totally occupied and totally free at the same moment. For someone feeling troubled, it can be wonderfully soothing—almost a form of therapy. As Sullivan's mind became focused, he felt lifted beyond his loneliness and worry.

He was just tossing a club when Frederick walked back again, the ironing board still under his arm.

"Oooh, I'm sure your mommy would be impressed."

Sullivan caught the clubs and turned to face him. The soothing feeling had instantly evaporated. "What's your problem, anyway?"

"My problem? You're my problem. You don't belong here. With us. We're real performers. And what are you? Nothing."

"Well, I don't even *want* to be here. I don't want to be one of you. And I'm not nothing. And I don't care what you think——"

But Frederick had continued on with a wave of his hand. Sullivan was left shaking with anger. What did he ever do to Frederick? Did he *ask* to be kidnapped? Because that's exactly what had happened to him. This was no accident. He was kidnapped and he was a prisoner and he hated it and wanted to go home.

Sullivan shoved his equipment into his backpack. He picked it up and strode toward the caravan. But then Clarence, who was sitting under a tree with the dogs, said, "Hey, Dexter. Sit down a minute."

"No, thanks."

"Come on. Take a load off."

Sullivan stopped. "My dad used to say that."

"Mine, too."

Sullivan walked over to him and sat on the ground. Clarence said, "You can't let Frederick get to you. He's just a jerk. And he wouldn't have said anything if you weren't good."

"I don't think so."

"I'm serious. He hates competition. He's always

judging who gets the most applause. And he sees that you're talented. Raw, sure, but talented. It gets his blood boiling."

"I hate him."

"I don't think I hate him. I feel sorry for him."

"Sorry?"

"Magic is the only thing he has." Clarence paused, a pained expression on his face. "Oh, jeez, what did these dogs eat? They're so gassy today. Maybe that should be in the act. *Clarence and His Amazing Farting Dogs.*"

Sullivan laughed. Snit and Snoot immediately jumped on him, licking his face and knocking him over.

❁

Each night the show began at dusk, the kerosene lamps illuminating the stage. And each show was a little bit different in feeling. Sometimes it was the audience, more talkative one night, more silently attentive the next. Sometimes it was a performer—Frederick glaring even more angrily than usual, or Esmeralda more comic or more elegant. On most nights somebody tried something new, to make his or her act better and, as Clarence told him, because doing the exact same thing got boring after a while. Sullivan never tired of watching, though. He didn't want to envy the others on the stage, not when they were all here against their will; didn't want to covet the applause of the crowd, the praise of Master Melville. But he couldn't help it.

After the show — after the excitement faded away and the night grew silent — was the worst time. The time that missing his mother and father and Jinny hurt like the deepest wound. But even this he started, slowly, to become used to. The pain itself became a kind of comfort to him as he lay on his bunk and felt the rhythm of the caravan's wheels. And he learned to fall asleep this way, easily and without dreams.

One evening near the end of his second week, as Sullivan helped Clarence pick up trash after the performance, a girl came up to them and said, "I liked the show. It's the best thing I ever saw, even better than the Ice Capades."

Clarence looked around a moment, as if to see whether they were being watched. The Melvilles were still busy selling Hop-Hop Drops at the table beside the caravan. "Thank you," he said. The girl was very tiny, even smaller than Clarence, with straight bangs and large eyes and a tiny nose. She was also very talk-ative. "I don't know what I liked better, the magic or the dogs or the tightrope," she went on. "And the lady who plays the music! She's beautiful, isn't she? But kind of scary. She never smiled once. I wish I played an instrument. Or had a dog. We've only got chickens and cows and a goat. But I'm really good at chess. I'm the school chess champion. My name's Lillian. Lillian Reilly. But everyone calls me Lilly. I wanted to play chess with Napoleon, but the man didn't pick me. Do you think he decided I was too young? I'm not as young as I look. I'm eleven. I'm just small. Which is strange, because my brothers and sisters are all big. I'm the runt of the litter, my dad says. He's the one who taught me to play chess but now I can beat him, too."

Lilly certainly was a talkative girl, thought Sullivan.

"Listen, Lilly," Clarence said, almost in a whisper. He glanced over his shoulder and then slipped his hand into his pocket. From it he drew out an envelope. Sullivan saw that it had an address and a stamp on it. "Could you mail this for me? It's to my parents." Lilly took it from him. "It would mean a lot to me . . ."

Clarence stopped. Sullivan had felt it, too—a narrow hand on his own shoulder. He turned to see Mistress Melville standing behind them, her long black hair framing her pale face. "Why, there's no need to bother the girl," she said, smiling coldly. "I'll be glad to mail your letter."

She released her grip on Sullivan, reached between them, and snatched the envelope from the girl's hand.

She held it to her breast, tapping her long nails against it. "Now run along, child. I'm sure your parents are waiting for you. We've got a lot of work to do here."

Then she grabbed Sullivan and Clarence by the collar and pulled them away. As they approached the caravan she hissed at Clarence, "You've been warned before. You don't talk to people. And you certainly don't write letters. But a warning wasn't good enough, I see. You need to be taught a lesson."

"I won't do it again, I won't! I was stupid. And . . . and ungrateful. I'm sorry."

"Yes," Sullivan pleaded. "He's sorry —"

"And he's going to be even more sorry in a minute. You, go and help the others," she ordered, putting her hand against Sullivan's back and giving him a hard shove.

He did as he was told. Clarence was made to sit by one of the caravan's wheels. When the caravan was packed up and the beds down, he was sent inside with Sullivan and the others without the usual evening snack. They changed under their covers, and Sullivan saw that Clarence was trembling. They lay in bed in silence and as Master Melville locked the door from the outside, Sullivan could hear him speaking to Mistress.

"Not too harsh now, my dearest. He is just a small boy. He's not that strong, you know."

"Don't be so pathetic," came Mistress Melville's voice. "It disgusts me. He must be made an example. To the others, and especially to the new boy. Now hurry up."

Sullivan listened, but there were no more voices. The horse whinnied as always and the caravan began to move.

"Maybe it won't be so bad," Sullivan whispered. "I mean, she is human, isn't she?"

But no one else said anything, not Esmeralda with soothing words or even Frederick, who might have been expected to tell Clarence how stupid he had been. The caravan rattled on, and even in the dark Sullivan knew that no one was asleep. They had traveled for nearly an hour when the caravan slowed. The wheels ground against gravel and stopped. A moment later came the key in the lock, and the door opened.

"You!" Mistress Melville said, pointing at Clarence. "Out."

Clarence slipped out of bed. He stood in his pajamas, his feet bare. A damp gust of wind swirled in. Clarence walked slowly to the door and stepped down beside her. Mistress Melville held a chain, which she wound around one of his wrists and locked. Then they began to walk away, Clarence with his head down. Through the open door, Sullivan and the others watched them go.

And then Sullivan saw what they were walking toward.

A cemetery.

The caravan had pulled up to a small, old cemetery. Behind a rusting fence were gravestones, their corners worn by decades of rain and wind, leaning this way and that. A cemetery in the middle of nowhere, surrounded by trees that must have died from some blight, for they had no spring leaves. Sullivan could see the two figures step over the broken gate. He saw Mistress point and Clarence hesitate a moment before he lay down on a gravestone that had fallen over. Mistress attached the other end of the chain to something—a broken piece of the iron fence, perhaps. Then she walked back, looked through the doorway at the rest of them, and shut the door. They heard the sound of the lock. Then they were moving again.

"We can't be leaving him there," Sullivan whispered. "In a cemetery! And do you hear that? It's starting to rain. We can't leave Clarence."

"There isn't anything we can do," Frederick said glumly. Esmeralda just lowered her head.

At Halloween, children like dressing as ghosts and goblins. They like putting Styrofoam gravestones on their lawns, plastic ghouls on their porches. But a real cemetery at night, with dead people moldering in the ground or already reduced to a pile of bones, and the cold, clammy feel of the stones, was nothing like Halloween. Sullivan couldn't sleep. Not with the image of Clarence lying there. What if he was found by wild animals? Or a grave robber? And while Sullivan didn't exactly believe in ghosts, he didn't have any proof to the contrary, either. What if the spirits of the dead really did come out at night? What if Clarence was so frightened that it made his heart stop?

It was clear from the turning and sighs in the other bunks that nobody else was sleeping, either.

And the caravan rolled on.

It was many long hours before the faintest light could be seen through the cracks in the walls. And another hour still before the caravan came to a halt. Some time after that, Sullivan heard the key in the padlock and then squinted against the sudden light as the back door was flung open.

"All right, my dears. Rise and shine," said Master Melville, a little less energetically than usual. "No dawdling, now. Time to make breakfast."

They all got up, dressed under their covers (Sullivan was becoming quite good at it), and stumbled out into the morning. Master Melville whistled as he set up the camping stove, but Sullivan thought that he was covering up his own worry about Clarence.

He had dark circles under his eyes, and when he said, "Why don't we have pancakes, eh?" Sullivan could see that his smile was forced.

"Hey," Frederick said under his breath as he walked past the others. "Soggy's gone."

Indeed, the horse was not in his harness or anywhere nearby. And when the pancakes were ready and they all gathered at the table, Mistress Melville did not come out of the caravan to sit at the head of the table.

"She's gone to get him," Frederick whispered.

"What's that?" said Master Melville testily. "No whispering, now. Eat up."

But Master Melville himself did not touch his breakfast. He looked off into the distance, his jaw grinding as if he were chewing invisible gum. At last he said, "Perhaps I should say a word or two." He looked at them now, from one to another. "Rules are there for a reason. They protect us, you see? All of us. Discipline is also there for a reason. We are a company of performers. Members of an honorable profession. We hold on to something of value, great value. We exist out of time, far from the noise of the contemporary world. This is why we delight our audiences. This is why we bring — I am not ashamed to say it — a little happiness. But what we have, what we *do*, is fragile. Make no mistake, it is easily broken. Any one of you can destroy what we have made. I know that. Mistress Melville knows that. Perhaps Mistress and I have different ways sometimes, but our goals are identical. And we do not waver in them. Or in our deep concern for each and every one of you. You are our family. That's right, our family. And now, finish eating. Dexter, you haven't touched your pancakes. Go on, you all need your strength."

But Sullivan couldn't eat. When breakfast was done, they began cleaning up. Sullivan still did not quite understand the rotation of jobs, and someone always had to tell him what to do. Today he was drying dishes while Esmeralda washed. He tried to ask her about Clarence, but she just held up her hand, as if to say, *No, please, I just can't speak.*

In fact, nobody spoke at all. Not all morning, or into the afternoon. And nobody did much of anything else, either; no practicing or cleaning equipment or even reading a book. Esmeralda sat on a tree stump and stared. Frederick leaned against the back of the caravan, switching a tree branch against the ground. Even Master Melville didn't do anything except sit in a folding chair under a tree with his hat on and his eyes closed.

And then, in the middle of the afternoon, Sullivan heard it. So did the others. Hoofbeats. Esmeralda stood up. Frederick dropped his branch. Master Melville put the folding chair by the caravan. And all of them stood and waited.

The horse appeared at the top of a low, distant hill. It was moving at a gallop but it still took some time before the figure really grew larger; before Sullivan could make out Soggy's ears and nose. And Mistress Melville, leaning forward, her arm snapping a riding crop against Soggy's side.

At last the horse was upon them and Mistress Melville pulled up on the reins. Her black attire was covered in a fine dust, as was her face. Only when the horse swung around did Sullivan see Clarence clinging to her from behind, his face in a grimace, his eyes closed as if he was somehow able to hold on while asleep or unconscious.

"Easy now — let's help the boy off," said Master Melville. He had to pry Clarence's fingers from Mistress Melville's waist, but as soon as he did, Clarence slumped backwards and would have fallen to the ground if Frederick hadn't caught him. Then Master Melville picked him up and carried him into the back of the caravan. Mistress Melville snapped, "Take care of the horse," then dropped the reins and retreated into the front part of the caravan.

"Water!" Master Melville called through the open

back door. "And then some soup broth. Warm, not hot."

Esmeralda ran to get the plastic water jug and hurried back with a tin cup of water. She came out sniffling and went to the stove that Frederick had already brought out. "He's very weak," she began. "But he opened his eyes. And do you know what he said? He said, 'I didn't see a single ghost.' And then he tried to laugh, but he couldn't."

Sullivan took care of Soggy. He brought him a bucket of water, which the horse noisily slurped up, and then an armful of hay. While Soggy ate, Sullivan wiped down his steaming flanks. When the soup was warm, Esmeralda carried it into the caravan while Sullivan waited outside, standing beside Frederick. It didn't matter that they didn't like each other, not now.

"The Mistress, she's gone too far," Frederick said.

Esmeralda came out and took the brush from Sullivan, then went to speak quietly to the horse. At last Master Melville came out, rubbing the side of his face with his hand.

He spoke to them, although he did not look directly at any of them. "The boy is all right. He needs to sleep. Let . . . let that be a lesson to everyone."

He said the words as if his heart wasn't in them.

THE LOCK

CLARENCE was allowed to lie in bed for the rest of the day and sit quietly behind the caravan during the evening performance, but the following evening he was back in the show again. Sullivan was so shaken up by what Mistress had done, and so frightened that something similar might happen to him, he became even more determined to get away. If all that was stopping him was the padlock on the door of the caravan, then he would find a way to break it.

His first thought was to disable the lock somehow,

maybe by sticking mud into it when it was open. But Master Melville would see the blockage as soon as he tried to lock it. Then Mistress would demand to know who did it, and Sullivan didn't know if he'd be able to prevent himself from looking guilty.

Was there some way to get a duplicate key? he wondered. But no, that wouldn't work. The lock was on the *outside* of the door.

For an entire day Sullivan pondered the question. And then, as he passed the back of the caravan late the next afternoon, he realized that it wasn't just the padlock that kept the door secure. Because the lock had to, well, lock onto something. And that something was a loop of metal—or rather two of them, each welded to a flat piece, one of which was screwed to the back of the caravan, the other to the frame of the door. When the door was closed the two loops lined up and Master Melville slipped the lock through them.

And if one of those pieces of metal came off? The door would open!

As soon as the idea came to him, he had to set the table for dinner. By the time he got another chance to examine the loops, it was too dark to see well enough. He had to wait until the next day, and a time when neither of the Melvilles might be looking to see what he was up to. He didn't want any of the other kids to see, either. Frederick might tell on him, and Essy and Clarence might try to stop him, thinking that trying to escape was too dangerous.

When he did, finally, get to look closely, he saw that the flat plate welded onto each loop was attached by two screws. Except that the plate on the door was already missing one screw. Which meant he only had to remove the other screw.

Which meant he needed a screwdriver.

Master Melville had a toolbox, but he kept it on his side of the caravan and there was no way Sullivan could get to it. So he kept his eyes on the ground for something that he might be able to use. Over the next few days he found a nail, a bit of twisted wire, and part of a broken zipper, but none of them worked as a screwdriver. And then, cleaning up after a show, he saw something glint between blades of brown grass. It was a pair of nail clippers, one of those little silvery contraptions with a chain on it and also a tiny nail file that swiveled out. The file felt thin enough, and strong enough, too. He slipped it into his pocket, but he didn't get a chance to try it out for the rest of that day. The next day he kept it hidden in his hand and then paused behind the caravan to try the screw.

It turned!

"Why are you dawdling about?" cried Master Melville. "Help with the curtain, will you?"

Every time he passed, Sullivan turned the screw a rotation or two. And slowly it came out of the door. But then he turned it one too many times and the screw and the piece of metal both fell from the door to the ground!

Sullivan searched frantically through the grass. He found the metal loop but he couldn't find the screw. When he saw Mistress out of the corner of his eye, he stood up quickly and shoved the loop into his pocket. Master Melville would see it was gone as soon as he went to lock the door that night. Sullivan felt the blood drain from his face. He didn't want to be left in a cemetery or have some other awful thing happen to him! He had to think, he had to think!

But he couldn't think, not of a single thing. The stage was ready, the lanterns lit. Sullivan saw the first mark approaching in the distance. His heart beat wildly in his chest. He would have to stick the metal piece on with something. With glue? But he had no glue. With chewing gum? He had no chewing gum, either.

But he knew where there was a piece.

A very old piece. An old, already chewed, dried-up

piece. It was stuck to the side of his fold-down bed; he had felt it once with his hand. Who knows what other kid had put it there. All Sullivan had to do was pull it off, chew it to make it soft (hoping that he didn't catch the bubonic plague or some other disease), and stick it on the back of the metal piece. The only problem was that he couldn't get to his bed—it had been folded up to allow the stage to come down. He would have to wait for the stage to go up again—in other words, until the very last moment.

Sullivan did not enjoy watching the show that night. He kept putting his hand in his pocket and feeling the metal piece and imagining what the Melvilles would do if they found it missing. When the show was finally over he made so many mistakes as he helped to take down the stage that Frederick and Master Melville both snapped at him in irritation.

And then at last they were in the caravan and changing under their covers. Sullivan only pretended to get out of his clothes. Then he reached over to the side of his bed, feeling along the edge until he touched the hardened lump of gum. He needed to use the nail file to pry it off. He grimaced in the dark and put it in his mouth. It tasted musty and cobwebby and without a hint of whatever flavor it had once been. It hurt his teeth to try and chew it, but after a minute or two it finally began to soften. He chewed and chewed until it was ready and then he plastered it on the bottom of the metal piece, as flat as he could make it. He threw off his covers and hurried up the aisle between the beds.

"Where are you going?" Clarence asked.

But Sullivan didn't answer. Instead, he stepped outside and peered closely at the door to see the mark in the paint where the metal piece had been before. He stuck it on, pushing hard. Then slowly he drew away his fingers.

The gum held.

"And just exactly what are you doing?" Master Melville asked.

Sullivan jumped. "I'm sorry. I just really have to, ah, pee one last time."

"You know that you're allowed to go before you change and not again."

"I know. I'm sorry."

"All right. But don't go too far. I want to be able to see you. Just turn your back, please."

"Yes, Master Melville."

Sullivan walked away from the caravan until he reached the trees. He turned his back and tried to go, but the truth was he was too scared. So he just pretended and then came back.

"Hurry up. To bed with you. And what are you doing still in your clothes? Get changed."

Sullivan scampered into bed, pulling the covers over himself. He held his breath and listened, afraid the metal piece would fall off. But sure enough, he heard the sliding of the key and then the click of the lock. It held! A moment later the caravan began to move. He knew that the others would be asleep in moments — they were always tired from the show, and the turning of the caravan's wheels was like the hypnotizing tick of a clock to them. Esmeralda was right — sleep was a gift.

Sullivan waited a while longer, just to be sure, until at last he could wait no more and slipped his feet out of bed and into his running shoes. He heard Clarence's wheezy breathing and a snore from Frederick. Snit and Snoot, lying on the end of Clarence's bunk, looked up at him and he patted their heads to settle them. Then he stood at the back of the caravan, took a breath, and pushed on the door. Immediately the metal piece pulled off and the door swung open.

Sullivan felt the cold air on his face as he looked down at the moving dirt road. A line of evergreens on either side of the road receded behind them. He set his jaw, grabbed the edge of the door frame, and pushed himself out.

The ground came up and hit him hard. He rolled over and over in the dust, and when he stopped he was on his back. He opened his eyes and saw the moon.

14

YELLOW EYES

FOR someone who has been deprived even for a short time, the sudden experience of freedom can feel strange and even disconcerting. First, there is disbelief. Are the shackles really off? Am I no longer being watched? Then, a delirious joy. But after that comes fear. Of being alone. And unprotected. Of having to make decisions that could turn out disastrously.

The landing stunned Sullivan. He sat up in the dirt road, catching his breath and listening as the sound of the caravan's wheels grew fainter and fainter. He could not believe his plan had really worked. Surely the Melvilles would swoop down on him at any moment. But nothing happened and slowly a sensation of wonder came over him. He could feel himself grinning in the dark. He was free; he could go home again. He would see his mother, his father, his sister. But after that came another, more unnerving sensation. He was in a strange place, in the dark. A moment ago he had at least had Clarence and Esmeralda and even Frederick for company, and all of them were in the same situation. But now he was as alone as he'd ever been in his life.

He got up, dusted himself off, and rubbed his shoulder where he had first hit the ground. He looked around and decided on another dirt road that branched off to the left. Maybe he would see a house or a farm —some lighted window he could walk toward.

But as he started out he saw nothing, only the dark shapes of trees. An owl hooted. He walked for fifteen minutes, a half hour, an hour, and after that he lost all sense of time. He was plodding along, not even trying to see anymore, when a swarm of small insects encircled him, fluttering against his face.

"Get away, get off!" he cried, waving his hands at them, hurrying forward. But they followed him like a cloud, one of them stinging him on the neck. Another pushed its way into his mouth and he struggled to spit it out. And then there was something else—larger, black things flittering close by but not quite touching him. Bats. They were feeding on the insects around his head.

"Ahhhhhh!"

Sullivan covered his face with his hands and started to run. He might still have been screaming, he wasn't sure; he knew only that he had to get away from these awful things. He ran flat out with his hands over his eyes, not caring where he was going.

Until he hit something. *Smack!*

Sullivan collapsed to his knees, moaning. He had gone forehead-first into a large object—not a tree. It was harder than a tree. His head rang. He couldn't breathe. He stayed on his knees until he could finally suck in a little air. The pain lessened to an awful throb and then he felt something warm and wet on his face. He touched his forehead with his hand. It was sticky. He put his finger to his tongue and tasted his own salty blood. He lay down in the dirt.

He knew he couldn't stay there and so he made himself stand up. He felt shaky, but he didn't go down again. He stepped toward whatever he had run into, slowly this time, with his hands outstretched. And touched rock. A sheer rockface, rising straight up from the ground. The road, he could just barely see, veered to the right. He wished that he could have a drink of water; his mouth was so dry. He took some slow, deep breaths and began walking again.

He didn't know how long he trudged on. It was still dark. His feet hurt and he had pains in the backs of his legs and he had a terrible thirst.

Listening carefully, he thought that he heard a trickling sound.

Water. To get closer to it, he went off the road, through sharp bushes that scratched his hands and face. But there it was, a small brook. The sound he had heard was the water running over rocks. It was the most beautiful music in the world. Sullivan leaned down and put his face to the water and sucked it up noisily. He'd never tasted anything better. He put his whole face and then his head in the water, and when he sat up again he let it drip down his back. He drank again. And then he looked up and saw two yellow eyes staring at him.

"Hello?" Sullivan said.

The eyes growled. Sullivan's heart pounded. The first thing he thought was: Wolf. But then he remembered that there weren't a lot of wolves left except in uninhabited places, so maybe it was a dog. A dog that had no home and had gone wild. The eyes came closer, and then he could just see the outline of a snout and the glint of teeth as it gave a low snarl. Backing up, Sullivan felt the scratchy bushes behind him. To push his way through them he would have to turn around.

"Please, please leave me alone," Sullivan pleaded softly. "Just go away, doggy."

The animal leaped. Its heavy paws came down on Sullivan's shoulders, knocking him backwards into the bushes. It snapped its jaws, grazing his neck. Sullivan felt its hot breath even as he reached out to push at its thick neck, trying to hold it off. But it was far too heavy and too strong and Sullivan shut his eyes, not wanting to see its teeth sink into him.

There was a yelp and squeal and then the animal was being pulled off him. He heard a thump and growl and then the pounding of the dog's running feet. Sullivan lay in the bushes, his cheek searing from a tear in the skin. He couldn't move, too exhausted from the fear draining away. Then he felt a hand. A woman's long, narrow fingers holding his own and then pulling him onto his feet.

"There, there, it's all over. No need to worry anymore. I have saved you. Yes, I've saved your life."

Mistress Melville. Sullivan could not stop himself from grabbing her around the waist as he began to sob.

She patted him lightly on the head. "There, there," she said again. "That's enough." She pried him off.

The caravan wasn't far away; they must have turned back to find him. Mistress led him by the hand and at the caravan door she used a damp towel to wash away the blood. She put a bandage on his head. She took him inside and tucked him into his bunk, leaning over so that her lips almost touched his ear. "We're your family now. Let us take care of you." Then she was gone and he felt the caravan's wheels turn.

He couldn't keep his eyes open.

❋

It took him a long time to wake in the morning. He heard whispering but only gradually could he make out the words.

"You're a traitor, Frederick, that's what you are."

"You think you know everything. And if I hadn't said anything? What would have happened to him, Clarence? He'd have been torn apart, that's what."

"But you didn't know that. For all you knew, he was already in contact with his parents."

"Of course he wasn't. Besides, what do you think would have happened to the rest of us if he had gotten away? What would they have done to us, eh? Worse than lying in some old cemetery, I'll tell you that. Do you think he worried about us before taking off? No, he only cared about himself. You should be thanking me."

"Thanking you? That's a joke. Admit it: you actually want to be here. You look up to them. And Mistress has you wrapped around her little finger. All she has to do is speak to you in a certain tone of voice."

"I don't know what you're talking about, but if you know what's good for you, you will shut right up—"

"That's enough from the both of you! We've all got to help each other the best we can. Now hush up and let him sleep."

"I'm not sleeping," Sullivan said, turning over. "I'm awake now."

Esmeralda slipped out of bed and came to his side. She ran her hand through Sullivan's hair. "Are you all right, Dex? There's a spot of blood coming through your bandage. You had a pretty rough time."

"I'm all right. I'm sorry if I made things harder. I was going to tell the police about all of you."

"Of course you were," Clarence said. "We're not worried about ourselves. It's you we're concerned about."

"I sure wouldn't like to be you right now," Frederick said. "None of us has actually tried to run. They must be thinking up some pretty severe punishment."

"Don't scare him," scolded Esmeralda. She turned

back to Sullivan. "Whatever happens, we'll help you. You'll get through it."

"That's right," Clarence said. "You'll get through it."

But he sounded doubtful. Sullivan hadn't wanted to consider the consequences of getting caught. What exactly were they going to do to him?

At that moment he heard the key in the lock—the door must have been fixed. When it opened, bright daylight filled the interior.

"Morning, dear children," said Master Melville. "Rise and shine. Today is a special day." He stepped up and into the caravan.

"Why?" Esmeralda asked. She had still been kneeling by Sullivan's bunk, but now she stood up. Master Melville came over and looked down at Sullivan. He said slowly, "Because of our Dexter."

"What are you going to do to him?" Clarence blurted out.

"Do? I'm going to let him begin his training. You see," he said, looking into Sullivan's eyes, "you must have a proper juggling routine, something really good, if you're going to join the show."

"I'm . . . I'm going to perform?" Sullivan said.

"Of course, dear boy. Isn't that, in your heart of hearts, what you really want?"

15

THE EMPTY DRAWER

No matter what Gilbert and Loretta Mintz felt, no matter how they suffered because of the loss of their son, they still had to keep running the Stardust Home for Old People. They had to get three meals a day in front of the forty-eight residents, had to wash dozens of bags of laundry, had to arrange for doctor visits and medication, for Scrabble tournaments and movie nights.

Not that anyone ate very much. Two weeks went by and still no one wanted to play Scrabble or watch a movie. For it wasn't just Sullivan's parents who grieved over his drowning. Every resident had known Sullivan well, had shared a joke with him, or had told him a story about the old days. Most kids think of old people as if they had always been old—as if they had been *born* old. But the truth is, their young selves still live inside them. Sullivan had been a rare boy, genuinely interested in hearing about their pasts, and for that they had all loved him. Seeing Sullivan had made them feel as if they were still a part of the world. As if they still mattered.

And now he was gone. Gilbert made fried chicken, almost everyone's favorite, and most of it remained on their plates. Loretta organized a Cary Grant movie night with decorations and popcorn (and softer treats for those with false teeth), and nobody came. It wasn't good for the health of the residents to be so depressed, but it was hard for Gilbert and Loretta to do much about it, given that they felt even worse.

And then there was Jinny. Sullivan's sister had reacted in a most alarming way. She pretended that Sullivan was still alive. She would say, "Let's make brownies. They're Sullivan's favorite." Or "We can't touch anything in Sullivan's room. It has to look just the same when he comes back." Or "I hope Sullivan comes home in time for my dance recital." Sullivan was almost all she ever talked about.

Hearing Sullivan's name so much was hard on his parents. But it was even worse to see Jinny living in a fantasy world. They let it go on for a while, for the thought of insisting on the truth was too painful, but soon it began to seem that this illusion might actually be harmful to her. Jinny had to come to terms with the way things really were. She had to accept that her brother was dead. And so one evening when she was ready for bed, they sat her on the sofa for a talk.

"We understand how hard it is to let go," said Loretta, holding her daughter's hand. "But we all have to face the sad, sad truth. Your brother is gone. He isn't coming back. And it's going to take a long time for the hurting to go away."

"But we'll always remember him," Gilbert said, taking her other hand. "We can talk about him whenever you want. Just not this way. You're so young. You've got your whole life ahead of you, Jinny. We want you to learn to be happy again. You have to try. We all have to try."

Jinny shook them off, stood up, and stamped her feet. "I won't try! I won't try!" Then she ran into her room and pulled her blanket over her head and cried. She wouldn't speak to either of them, and so they just stood in her doorway until, exhausted from crying, she finally fell asleep.

In the morning, Gilbert and Loretta went to Manny

Morgenstern's room to talk to him about Jinny. Even at eighty-one, Manny was the most active resident at the Stardust Home, although lately he had taken to staying in his room. He would stand at the window and look out on the street for hours. And that was how they found him when they knocked on his door.

"Jinny adores you," Loretta said. "And she knows that you were close to Sullivan. Maybe you could talk to her."

"We think she needs to hear it from somebody else," Gilbert said. "That Sullivan isn't coming back."

Manny looked at them. He ran his gnarled fingers through his sparse white hair. He stroked his bearded chin. "Yes," he said at last, "I'll talk to her."

❋

Life, thought Norval Simick, could sure be strange. Not long ago he had considered Samuel Patinsky his worst enemy. Maybe Samuel hadn't picked on him as much as he had Sullivan, but he had still insulted him, or pulled his chair out from under him, or tore his homework into bits.

And now Samuel wasn't doing any of that, not to Norval or anyone else. Well, Norval did see him pull a chair out from under a kid in History class, but then he helped the kid up and even apologized. It was as if he couldn't keep himself from doing it — like it was an old habit—but then was sorry he had. And since then, he hadn't been mean to anybody.

And here they were now, sitting in the lunchroom across from one another. Samuel was eating a salami sandwich and talking seriously about organizing a Sullivan Mintz Day.

"The thing is," Samuel was saying, "it can't be a downer. You know, all depressing because of what happened to Sullivan. It has to be a real celebration. Don't you think?"

"I agree," Norval said. "In fact, that's what we should call it. Not a memorial or anything like that. We should call it the Sullivan Mintz Celebration Day."

"That's genius," Samuel said. He chewed some more on his sandwich. "We have to take this to the principal."

"Samuel, can I ask you something?"

"Shoot."

"What's it feel like? Not, you know . . ."

"Not being a jerk?"

"Basically, yes."

"It feels weird, actually. I mean, okay, it's wrong to be a bully. But people knew who I was. I had a certain stature. If I'm not this guy everybody is afraid of, then who am I?"

"Wow." Norval nodded sagely. "You're having an identity crisis."

"You're right! I *am* having an identity crisis."

"I've heard about them, but I've never known any-one who actually had one."

"Neither have I," said Samuel. "I might even be the first in all of Beanfield. Pretty cool. Hey, but let's not get sidetracked here. We're talking about the Sullivan Mintz Celebration Day."

"Right. Maybe we should prepare a little more. Actually, a lot more. We have to make sure he doesn't turn us down."

Samuel was already getting up. "Then what are we waiting for? Let's get to work."

❁

Manny waited until he found Jinny alone in her room, sitting with her various dolls and stuffed animals in a circle, each with a toy teacup in front of it. There was one space open in the circle. Manny knew who the space had been left for.

"Hey there, Jinny," he said. "Mind if I join your tea party?"

"Okay," Jinny said. "But don't take Sullivan's spot. You can push Hoppy closer to Teddy-Poo. Just don't let them poke each other."

"Sure thing." He lowered himself with a groan. "Boy, it was easier sitting on the ground when I was just seventy," he said, trying to cross his legs. "You know, Jinny, I sure miss Sullivan."

"Me, too," said Jinny.

"I hear you think he's coming back."

"Yup. He went to see the doctor show."

"Yes, I heard about you telling that to your parents. They think you have a good imagination."

"I know what that means. They think I made it up. I didn't. There was a lady in black who played a big drum. And a man who sold bottles. And a girl who walked on the piperope. I saw it with Sullivan. He went to see them again, I know he did. That's where he is."

"Jinny, do you mean a medicine show?"

"That's what I said."

"I seem to remember Sullivan asking me something about medicine shows." Manny rubbed his goatee. "That's a bit odd."

"I can show you something," Jinny said.

"All right, then. Show me."

"You have to get up."

"You have to help me."

So Jinny helped Manny up from the floor, which wasn't too difficult as Manny was so thin that he weighed about as much as a stack of paper. Then she took his hand and walked him out of her room and into the hall.

"Where are we going?" Manny asked.

"Sullivan's room."

It was right beside Jinny's. The door was closed—it was always closed now—and Jinny opened it and then closed it again after she and Manny were inside. "I'm not supposed to come in here," she said, "because they think it will make me sad. But I like it in here."

Manny and Jinny looked around. They looked at the shelf of Peanuts comic books over the small desk. At the bulletin board crowded with photographs, funny drawings, and a ribbon with the word *Participant* on it that Sullivan had gotten for finishing second to last in a race. At the posters of famous jugglers. At some laundered clothes folded neatly on the dresser.

"I like it here, too," said Manny. "But what did you want to show me?"

"Oh, I almost forgot," Jinny said. "I want to show you this."

Jinny went over to the dresser and pulled out the bottom drawer.

Manny looked into it. "It's empty. It's an empty drawer."

"Exaply."

"But I don't see——"

Manny stopped. His heavy eyebrows knitted together. He looked from side to side and then back down. He said very quietly. "Jinny, quick now, go get your parents."

Manny stood and waited. He could hear Jinny calling and then Gilbert asking what was wrong and Loretta saying hold on a minute, her hands were covered in sugar, and a few moments after that the three of them came into Sullivan's bedroom. Jinny went right in, but her parents stopped in the doorway.

"Now, Jinny," said Gilbert. "We already told you that it's not a good idea to play in here."

"Come and see this," said Manny.

Gilbert and Loretta looked at each other. Loretta wiped her hands on her apron and the two approached, standing on either side of Manny. Jinny came up alongside her father so that the four of them were staring down.

"It's an empty drawer," said Gilbert.

"Yes," said Manny. "But what did Sullivan keep in there?"

"His juggling things," said Loretta.

"Right. And where are they now?"

"I don't know," said Loretta.

"They're with Sullivan! They're with Sullivan!" Jinny jumped up and down.

Manny said, "Why would he take all his juggling equipment? Even the instruction books."

"That's a good question," said Gilbert. "But what's the answer?"

"Because he must have thought he needed them," said Loretta.

"For the medicine show!" said Jinny. "That's what I said before."

Loretta put her hand to her mouth. "Gilbert," she said. "We have to call the police."

❁

It was nearly three hours before Officer Spoonitch and Officer Forka arrived at the Stardust Home. "We're very sorry," said Officer Spoonitch, wiping his feet on the mat, "but we were on another case. We're very short-staffed at the moment. A lot of our officers are home sick with the flu."

"I just got over it," said Officer Forka.

"We're glad you're here," said Gilbert. "We would like to show you something."

Soon there were six of them in Sullivan's room, all staring down.

"An empty drawer," said Officer Spoonitch, "isn't a very solid piece of evidence."

"But it's something," said Loretta. "It's a lead, isn't it?"

"A lead usually points us in a certain direction," said Officer Forka. "But this doesn't point anywhere."

"It points to Jinny telling the truth about the doctor—I mean the medicine show," Manny explained. "They just might have something to do with it. What did you say the full name was, Jinny?"

"I'm not sure. Master Marvel's Medicine Show. Or maybe Master Moorville. Or Mellrose."

Officer Spoonitch coughed. "I think I might be coming down with something now." He swallowed and felt his throat. "The case isn't officially closed since no body—since your son wasn't actually found. We'll see if these names turn up anything."

"Thank you," said Loretta.

Officer Spoonitch put his hand on his forehead. "I think I need to lie down."

❄

For four days Gilbert and Loretta waited to hear from the officers. At last, just after dinner, Officer Forka arrived at the door. While Gilbert, Loretta, Jinny, and Manny sat and listened, she apologized for the delay, saying that Officer Spoonitch was down with the flu and the police force was even more short-staffed. She had finally been able to search the police records and other directories but found no record of a Master Marvel, Moorville, or Mellrose. And there were no businesses anywhere listed as a medicine show. She had reached another dead end.

Officer Forka was not uncaring, and neither was she incompetent. Through long experience, she had learned that the great majority of crimes and accidents are not unusual or strange or even difficult to understand. If a boy goes missing and his jacket is found in the river, then it is almost certain that the boy has drowned. And while weird clues turn up in almost every case, in the end those clues usually don't matter. Officer Forka did not want to give the Mintzes bad news, but it was her duty to be honest with the family of a victim. It was also her duty to move on to cases that really did need solving. So Officer Forka said she was sorry and then got up and put on her cap and left.

For a long moment, none of them spoke. At last Gilbert said, "It was worth trying. Everything is worth trying." But he didn't sound as if he meant it.

"But what about the medicine show?" Manny asked.

"Sullivan loved to read about all those old entertainments. Circuses, vaudeville. I'm sure he liked to tell Jinny about them. But medicine shows don't exist anymore."

"You don't believe me?" Jinny protested.

Loretta turned and took Jinny's hand. "I believe absolutely that you wish your brother was still here."

Jinny pulled away. "I'm going to find my brother. That's all. I'm going out to find him."

She stood up and marched to her room. Her parents followed and watched as she packed a pair of socks, a sticker book, and a Kit Kat into a pillowcase. Then she marched downstairs, put on her pink fuzzy hat with pussycat ears, and went out the door.

They found her on the sidewalk. They made her come back inside.

The next day they found her three doors down.

The day after that they found her at the corner.

Gilbert said, "This isn't a game, Jinny."

"I know it isn't a game. I'm not playing piddly-binks, you know."

"I think we'd better have a family meeting," Loretta said.

"Yes, we better," Jinny agreed, folding her arms with determination. "Because I'm going to look for my brother and you can't stop me."

The meeting was held that evening after dinner. Jinny's parents asked Manny to come, too. Now that Sullivan was gone, he had become even more a part of their family.

"So here we are," Gilbert said. "And you know why, Jinny."

"Yes, I do. Because I am going to look for Sullivan."

"You're six years old, honey," said Loretta. "You can't leave on your own. You'll get lost. It isn't safe. There's really no room to negotiate on this point."

"Okay," Jinny said.

"Good," said Gilbert.

"Manny can go with me."

Loretta sighed. "Jinny, dear, Manny can't go with you. He's eighty-one years old. A very spry eighty-one, but still, that is really quite old. Forgive me for saying it, Manny."

"That's all right. I'm definitely old," Manny said.

"Please tell Jinny that you can't go with her. That we're all very sad, but it won't help if she runs away. Tell her she has to stop."

Manny considered a moment. He rubbed his chin. "I'll go," he said.

"What?" exclaimed Gilbert.

"Jinny and I will go look for Sullivan. You see, Gilbert, Loretta, I think she needs to. I think she'll never get over it if she doesn't."

"That's right, I'll never get over it," said Jinny.

"What are you saying, Manny?" Loretta cried. "This is crazy. This is irresponsible."

Manny said, "I feel very well these days. I've got my pension money to keep us going if we're careful. I can even give Jinny some lessons while she's away from school, teach her how to read. Give us two weeks. If we don't find something definite in that time, we'll come home."

"That's right," Jinny said. "After two weeks. I'll even spit-shake on it."

Jinny spit on her hand and held it out to shake. Loretta began to cry quietly.

"Hooray!" said Jinny. "I'm going to look for my brother!"

16

THE DIRECTOR

$\mathcal{S}$ULLIVAN stood watching Frederick on the open grass. Behind Frederick ran a fence, and behind the fence stood four goats. The goats were watching Frederick too, and every so often one would *maa* in approval.

The older boy was talking aloud and gesturing while holding a length of rope in one hand and a large pair of scissors in the other. Sullivan had decided to approach him for help in creating his own act, since he seemed the most professional and polished of the performers. He was constantly rehearsing, learning new effects, even changing his patter.

Unfortunately, he was also Frederick. Cold, unfriendly, and mean. As Sullivan watched, he tried to work up his courage to approach him. Master Melville had told Sullivan again that it was time to create an act for himself and then had gone into town to get food and supplies. After his attempt to run off, Sullivan had been surprised and relieved not to be given some awful punishment, and he didn't want to anger Mistress Melville — who had, after all, rescued him — by refusing to perform. Going along with developing an act would encourage the Melvilles to believe that he had accepted his fate. They would stop watching him so closely and he could then find a better way to get free. And in the meantime, practicing would give him something to do. That he might actually *want* to create an act — that, he refused to believe.

But he just wasn't sure how to approach Frederick. At last Sullivan made himself walk toward him.

"Frederick, I was really hoping —"

"Ah, look what you made me do! I cut the wrong loop. You're a pest, Dexter."

"Yes, I'm sure I am, and I'm sorry about that. But I was really hoping, if it isn't too much trouble, that you might help me put my juggling act together. I mean, your own act is so great. It's really slick."

Frederick looked down at Sullivan. He narrowed his eyes. "Your compliments don't mean a thing to me. Do you think I would waste my time helping a hack like you? A total amateur? What do I care if you fall flat on your face? I'll enjoy hearing the audience boo you off the stage. Get lost."

He made a shooing motion with his hand. Sullivan backed away. It was hopeless. He turned around and saw Esmeralda. She was hanging some wash on a line strung from the door of the caravan to a rusting tractor. She wore a linen top and a peasant skirt and her hair fanned over her shoulders. Each of them was responsible for his own washing, something that Sullivan had never had to do before, and Esmeralda had patiently shown him how to get all the soap out of his clothes. Why hadn't he thought of asking her to help him?

"Hey, Essy," he said, walking over. "I was wondering if you could do me an awfully big favor."

Esmeralda turned around. "Sure, what is it?"

"I'm wondering if you could help me develop my juggling act. I don't have a clue what to do."

She nodded. "I remember that feeling. I'd love to,

Dex. There's only one problem. I wouldn't be very good at it. I needed help to figure out my own. I think I'd be a terrible director for somebody else."

"Who helped you?" Sullivan asked.

"The same person who helped Frederick. Clarence."

"Clarence? *Clarence* helped *Frederick*?"

"Not that Frederick would ever admit it. In fact, he pretends that Clarence only gave him a pointer or two. But it's not true. Clarence figured out all the important things—the tone, the feeling, the presentation. He's terrific. You should ask him."

"Okay." He watched her get back to hanging up her wash.

Sullivan walked past a pile of big rocks that had been pulled out of the field by some farmer a long time ago. He went to find Clarence on the other side of the caravan. Clarence was washing, too—only he was washing Snit and Snoot. He had a basin of soapy water and was scolding the two little dogs for jumping into the tub and then onto him, covering him with soapsuds.

"That looks like fun," Sullivan said.

"It isn't after you've done it a few hundred times. They rolled in something by the creek and came back stinking. There's nothing these two like better than to smell disgusting. Maybe I should try washing them as part of the act."

"I bet you could make it work," Sullivan agreed. "You've already done a lot for me, Clarence. I really appreciate it. But I need somebody to help me with my act. I don't even know how to start. Or what to say. What sort of person to be on stage. Essy told me how you helped her and Frederick. I know I don't have a lot of talent and I'm just an amateur, but if I don't try, the Melvilles are going to make things worse for me."

Clarence wiped some soapsuds from his face. "Let me check my schedule," he said. "I've got a business meeting at ten. Then a massage. After that I've got to meet with a television producer. But I might have some time after that."

"Oh, sure."

"Dexter, I'm kidding. Of course I'll help you. Anyway, I like doing it — it's something I'm good at. Could you grab that other towel and dry Snoot? Then we can get started."

Drying Snoot, it turned out, was like trying to gift-wrap a seal. Sullivan got wetter as the dog got drier, but at last it was done. He went into the caravan, picked up his backpack, and brought it over to Clarence and laid out the equipment: two sets of balls, three clubs, and the rings. He remembered exactly where and when he'd bought them, how he had saved his allowance. He remembered his hours of practicing in his room and how Manny would stand in the door and watch him. All of that seemed like a long time ago. The terrible taste of homesickness swelled in his throat, but he swallowed it down and asked Clarence how they should start.

The first thing that Clarence asked was to simply see what Sullivan could do. He started with three balls, moving from the basic cascade to the more complicated moves and finally adding the fourth ball. After that he used the rings and clubs, although his routines with each of them were more limited. He never fully got in the groove, but he didn't mess up too much. He did well enough to give Clarence a good idea of his abilities.

"I need a few minutes to think," Clarence said. He began to pace back and forth, head bent down, scratching at his nose. Just when Sullivan thought he couldn't take the waiting any more, Clarence sat on the grass. Sullivan joined him.

"Okay," Clarence said. "Let's take stock of what we've got here. Your skills are pretty decent for an amateur. You've got pretty much the standard set of juggling moves, maybe a bit extra, but nothing really fancy. There's a lot of repetition — the same moves, just with different objects. There's nothing that could be a climax to the show. But there's a good base to work from. First, we'll want to get your throws higher to make them more dramatic. Also cleaner and crisper. Then we'll need to add some showier stuff, which will take practice. And we'll have to find a way to get each routine to connect to the next, like scenes in a story."

Sullivan listened. It seemed like an awful lot to do. Maybe more than he was capable of. But he said, "Okay, I'm willing to try."

"Oh, and of course there's the most crucial thing," Clarence said.

"What?"

"Your personality."

"I need a personality?"

"Definitely. Frederick wouldn't be half as mesmerizing if he didn't have that snooty, ain't-I-better-than-you attitude. It makes him seem larger than life, kind of like royalty. When he started, he was trying to be friendly with the audience, trying to be funny — man, is he terrible at telling jokes. And Essy, she was doing straight ballet stuff. Elegant, but also pretty boring. But when she wasn't rehearsing for the show she'd goof around, do all these weird jumps and moves and twirls that she made up. I just suggested that she put them in the act. You see, your stage personality has to be something authentic, something that comes from who you are."

Snit and Snoot rambled over, Snoot nudging Sullivan under the arm to be patted. Sullivan rubbed her ears. He could see that Clarence was right. The only problem was, he had no idea what sort of stage personality he ought to have. What sort of personality did he have now? Did he have any personality at all?

Sullivan said, "I'm not funny. And I'm not snooty. And I'm not mysterious, either. I don't think there's anything special about me."

"Of course there is," Clarence said. "It just isn't as obvious as for someone like Frederick. We'll figure it out. Tell you what, Dex: We'll just start with the routines. Work on them and let the personality come after. I think we should begin with balls because you're best at them. We'll work your different moves into a flowing routine with some highlights so people can clap, and come up with an exciting finish. And then we can move on from there. Sound all right?"

"Sounds good," Sullivan agreed, although he felt doubtful. Doubtful about everything.

❊

They worked every day. First Clarence would help Sullivan figure out a series of moves. A sequence might begin modestly and then grow and grow until it *seemed* as if Sullivan was going to lose control (but he actually had to be fully *in* control), and then climax in a shower of high throws followed by dramatic catches. Or it might grow quickly, quiet down again, then grow, back and forth, ending in a totally unexpected move like a series of spins or over-the-shoulder, under-the-leg throws. The point, Clarence said, wasn't just to juggle well but to create a drama, with rises and falls, moments that were like whispers and others that were full of excitement. "I want the audience to worry about you," he said. "To think you're going to drop everything or get bonked on the head. I want them to feel as if their concentration is somehow helping you. I want them to be *involved*. I want them to be committed."

Sullivan had certainly never thought of such things when he was learning to juggle. He had thought it was enough just to keep the objects in the air without dropping them. But Clarence even choreographed a moment where Sullivan dropped a ball as if by mistake. And then, while keeping the other two in the air, he had to struggle to pick it up with his foot. Dropping one, Clarence said, would show the audience that he wasn't perfect, that he might fail at any time. That would make them root for him. And picking it up again would give them a chance to cheer encouragement.

Once the routines were set, Sullivan had to practice them over and over. If one part gave him trouble, then he had to practice just that for a stretch. It was hard and tiring work. He was only too glad when dinner came, for all that practice gave him a ravenous appetite. And each night, watching the others perform from the wing, he had a new appreciation for their skills and talents. He saw now that they were also actors, each playing a character that the audience believed in. He was amazed at how they could make the audience hush with expectation or gasp in fear, or clap in relief and appreciation.

"Watch them, watch them, dear boy!" Master Melville whispered to him one evening. "Let them all be your teachers. Each has learned from experience. By *feeling* the reaction out there. Now they play the crowd like a fish on a line. Watch, and you'll see!"

✳ 17 ✳

ONE morning Sullivan woke up to find that the caravan had stopped beside a burned-out house. The shell of the house still stood but all the window and door frames were charred and the roof had collapsed. Through the broken windows he could see curling wallpaper and even a blackened table and chair. There was something sad and forlorn about the sight. He wondered what had happened to the family that used to live there.

Distracted by the house, Sullivan at first didn't

notice a tent he'd never seen before erected behind the caravan. It was an old canvas tent, the size
of a large shed, with painted images, chipped and
faded, of horses and clowns and trapeze artists on it.
Sullivan could just make out the ghostly words on
the side: *Mandoni's Miniature Circus — Half the Size,*
Twice the Fun.

No one else seemed to take notice of it; they all
just went about their business getting breakfast ready.
It was only when they were seated and had begun
to eat, without Master Melville joining them, that
Sullivan finally said something.

"Why is that tent up?" he asked.

Mistress looked sideways across the table at him.
"Somebody tell the boy." She sighed. "I certainly can't
be bothered."

Clarence said, "It's B and B Day."

"B and B Day?"

"Brewing and Bottling. Master Melville is making
up a new batch of Hop-Hop Drops. We must be almost out."

"He makes it himself?" Sullivan asked.

"Enough questions," Mistress said. "All this talk
hurts my head."

The rest of the meal passed in silence, but Sullivan
couldn't suppress his curiosity about the making of

Hop-Hop Drops. He had often wondered about them —what the ingredients were, how they were made, whether or not they actually worked. From a small hole cut near the top of the tent, smoke rose steadily into the pale sky. Every so often there was an odd sound of grinding or whirring, and once in a while Master Melville could be heard cursing to himself or suddenly crying out.

Clarence had assigned Sullivan the task of improving several moves in his club routine, moves that two weeks ago he hadn't been able to do at all. In one he had to lean his head back and balance a club on his nose. After ten seconds or so he had to drop his head forward, catch it, and begin juggling again. First he'd had to learn to get it onto his nose and balance it. Then he'd had to learn how to tip it off without losing control. And *then* he'd had to learn how to catch it and start throwing again. He could do each move by itself, but doing all of them in succession was really hard. Right now he could manage it maybe one out of three times. He had to be able to do it every time.

Sullivan fetched his backpack and chose a spot not far from the flap of the tent. He started to practice but he couldn't help listening to the sounds coming from the other side of the canvas. At this distance, he could hear a bubbling sound. Also mutterings. And then Master Melville stuck his head out the flap and began to shout:

"*Capsicum! I need capsicum!*"

"There's no need to shout," Mistress answered from under an elm tree where she had gone to brush her long black hair. "There's some in the caravan. I'll get it."

"No need to shout? Do you know what it's like in here? Do you understand the necessity of precise timing? Do you comprehend at all the danger of ignition, combustion, and conflagration? You do not, no, you do not!"

Sullivan had never heard Master Melville dare talk to his wife this way. He was always trying to appease and flatter her. And when he neglected to, Mistress Melville let him know it. But now all she did was go into the caravan, fetch an unmarked aluminum can, and put it into his hands.

"There now, don't get your knickers in a knot," she said mildly.

He didn't answer, but pulled himself quickly inside again. Mistress gave Sullivan a dark look and walked back to her place under the elm tree. Immediately he began to throw his clubs, wanting to look busy. He tried the balancing move, and bonked himself just above his eye.

It was a good half hour before Master Melville stepped out of the tent again, rubbing his hands on a cracked leather apron tied around his waist. "Ah, Dexter," he said, his voice sounding far more cheerful. "Bit tense in there sometimes. Bit agitating. Have a short break now, during the first brewing stage. It's really quite a process, I must say. A little of this, a pinch of that. Stir, heat, boil, cool, shake, boil again. And when the stuff is done it needs to age three weeks in the bottle. Tastes quite awful. Bitter. Acrid. Sour. Burning. And an aftertaste of sickly sweet. But if it didn't taste that way, it wouldn't do any good, would it?"

Sullivan nodded in agreement and asked, "Do you take it too, Master Melville?"

Master Melville frowned. "Do I look as if I need it? Do I appear to you anything but the picture of happiness? Could I be in anything but a state of bliss, married to such a woman as I am? Really, I'm offended at the very thought of it. Now get along with you—I've got much more work to do."

And he went back into the tent, pulling the flap closed behind him.

❧

Clarence still hadn't come up with a personality for him, but Sullivan kept practicing. He worked on juggling with crossed arms, and then uncrossing and crossing them again while keeping the balls in the air. His moves became sharper, more precise.

One day after breakfast Sullivan said, "What should we start with today? Rings?"

"No, none of the usual," Clarence replied, holding a burlap sack at his side. "You need something else. Something unusual and unexpected."

"Like what?"

"Like this."

From inside the sack, Clarence drew out . . . a toaster.

"Excuse me? I'm supposed to throw *that* in the air?"

"And this," Clarence said. He brought out a rubber boot.

"Yeah, right." Sullivan laughed nervously.

"Oh, and also this."

A piggy bank.

"Is that porcelain?" asked Sullivan. "Isn't it breakable?"

"Very breakable." Clarence smiled. "The crowd is going to love it."

"I can't juggle a toaster, a boot, and a piggy bank. The toaster will land on my head! You're crazy, Clarence. I won't do it."

Clarence tossed the toaster at him. Sullivan caught it clumsily against his stomach. "Shall we get started?"

It was almost like learning to juggle all over again. First, he started with just the toaster. Clarence took out the insides to make it lighter, and Sullivan tossed it from one hand to the other, getting used to the way it felt, how to wrap his fingers around it. Then he did the same with the boot, after Clarence stuffed it with rags to make it stiff and sewed it shut at the top. Finally, Sullivan tried the porcelain pig. Clarence brought out a mattress from the caravan for Sullivan to stand on so that if the pig fell it wouldn't break.

Sullivan threw it . . . and missed. It bounced off the mattress. The curly tail broke off.

Clarence looked at it lying there. "The tail would have just gotten in the way," he said.

Next came throwing two of the objects—first the toaster and the boot, then the boot and the pig, then the toaster and the pig. Only when he could do that easily did he try all three. And then try again. And then again. The hardest part was adjusting for the different weight and shape of each object, both when catching and throwing, first deliberately and then, in time, without having to think. But he did it. He learned to juggle a toaster, a boot, and a piggy bank.

"This is fun," Sullivan said, throwing and catching, throwing and catching. "But there's no way I'm going to try a spin."

"I didn't even ask you to," Clarence said.

"Fine. I'll try one. But if I don't make it the first time I'm not trying again."

"Whatever."

Sullivan threw the objects. He spun on his heel, 360 degrees. He caught them.

"Showoff," said Clarence.

✳

Lying in his bunk that night, even before the caravan began to move, Sullivan felt himself falling asleep. He started awake at the sound of the lock opening again.

The back door swung wide and Mistress Melville stepped in, holding a lantern that illuminated her face in a ghoulish way. "Never use a boy to do a woman's job," she said. "You, the one who juggles."

"Yes?" Sullivan said, sitting up. The others were all up too, and watching silently from their bunks.

"I've got it."

"Got what?" Sullivan asked.

"Your personality. For your act."

"You do? What is it?"

"I'll tell you tomorrow."

She stepped backwards out of the caravan and closed the door again, leaving Sullivan and the others in darkness.

18

THREE LEGS

MANNY Morgenstern told Jinny an old riddle. What creature begins its life walking on four legs, then uses two legs, and finally three legs? Jinny made a lot of guesses—a weird spider? A robot? But finally Manny had to tell her the answer: a human. First it crawls on all fours, then it learns to walk on two, and finally, growing old, it uses a cane. And then he took his own rather splendidly carved cane from his closet. It was the last thing he needed before he and Jinny set out to look for Sullivan.

"I need one, too!" Jinny cried, and ran to her room. She came back with a plastic red and white striped cane, like a big candy cane, with a squeaker on the end that made a noise whenever she set it down.

"Ready?" Manny asked, putting on his fedora.

"Ready!" said Jinny.

But Jinny's parents, Gilbert and Loretta, weren't ready. First, Loretta insisted that the two have an enormous breakfast of eggs and sausages and toast. In the morning edition of the *Beanfield Gazette* there was a new poem by the Bard of Beanfield. Jinny's dad insisted on reading it out loud.

> *To lose one kid is bad enough.*
> *In fact, there's nothing worse.*
> *But to have to watch a second leave*
> *Is truly a parent's curse.*

"Well, Mom," Jinny said brightly, "it's your shortest, but it's not your bestest."

Gilbert wanted to check that Manny had enough money in his money belt, and that Jinny, too, had money in a little pouch on a string around her neck. Also that Manny had the maps and the first-aid kit and the phone number of the police station. Loretta wished that they could afford a cell phone for the pair, but Manny assured her they would find pay phones and check in regularly. At last, Jinny's parents agreed that the two were ready to go. But not without a farewell first.

Outside the Stardust Home, forty-seven old people lined up: a row of wheelchairs in front and another row of people leaning on them behind. Jinny stood with her Kooky Kitty backpack and her toy walking stick and her straw hat. Manny had his own canvas army backpack with leather straps. In the doorway Gilbert and Loretta held on to each other, Gilbert sniffling and Loretta flat-out crying.

Manny raised his cane and turned to face the crowd. "Dear friends," he said. "We embark on this journey for one purpose and one purpose only. And that is to find our own wonderful boy, Sullivan. And if we don't find him, then to find out what happened to him. But Jinny here believes that Sullivan is out there somewhere, and I believe Jinny. Don't worry about us. We'll take care of each other, won't we, Jinny? And we'll keep in touch. Please don't be glum," Manny added, for to his dismay, people were beginning to cry all up and down the rows. "We've had our sad days. This is the beginning of happier times!"

"Hooray for us!" Jinny cried. "Hip hip, hooray!"

Lorretta stepped toward them and put her hands

on Jinny's shoulders. "Remember, you can come home anytime. And if it looks like you won't find Sullivan, don't be afraid to tell us. Just come back. You need to eat properly, and drink three glasses of milk a day. You too, Manny — you need the milk for those old bones of yours. Oh, I can't believe we've agreed to this."

"Now, now, Loretta," Manny said. "You act as if I've lived my whole life in the Stardust Home. I was an adventurous lad in my day. I traveled from here to there and back again, with hardly two pennies to rub together. I may be old, but I'm resourceful. We'll be just fine. Now, we'd better get going. Goodbye, Loretta, Gilbert. Goodbye, forty-seven! See you all soon!"

"Goodbye!" yelled the people gathered in front of the Home. "Good luck!"

Jinny hugged her parents hard. For the first time she, too, felt tears in her eyes. Wiping them away, she said, "Aw, Mom, you sure do a lot of cry-babbling."

"Yes, I do," Loretta agreed. Then she hugged Manny. Gilbert hugged Manny, too.

"Down the belly brick road!" cried Jinny. She hooked her arm with Manny's. And the two began marching forward, Jinny's cane squeaking each time it hit the ground.

❋

They walked and walked and Jinny did not look back until they were quite far away. When she did, she could still see them all, very small, lined up along the sidewalk. The sight made her heart hurt, and for the first time she felt scared. Where were she and Manny going? How long would they be gone? She believed that her brother was alive, but that didn't mean she knew where he was or how to look for him.

"Where are we going first?" she asked Manny.

"Well, I thought we'd better take a look at the river. I hope that won't be too hard for you, Jinny. It's where the last piece of evidence — Sullivan's jacket — was found. I don't know what we might learn there, but you never know."

"Okay." Jinny nodded. Ever since Sullivan had disappeared, she hadn't wanted to see the river. She hadn't wanted to go near it. But now she had to. The two of them walked on and on — it took them a good hour to reach the part of the river that flowed through Beanfield Park.

Here, it was calm and quiet, the grass trimmed neatly along the banks and pretty willow trees planted along the shore. But the spot where the police had found the jacket was farther along, after the park ended and a stretch of wild scrub began. Manny and

Jinny kept going, pushing through branches and brambles with their canes, getting scratched and poked at every step.

It took them a while to get to a small incline, where the ground was soft and moss-covered. They found the tree where, caught on a slender branch, Sullivan's jacket had been discovered. They knew it was the right tree because the police had said it had been hit by lightning. Just being there made Manny tear up. "Careful now," he said, using his cane as he made his way down. The moss felt spongy underfoot.

"What do we look for?" Jinny asked. Her voice trembled.

"I don't know," Manny admitted.

Just then Jinny felt a drop on her nose. Then another on her cheek. "It's starting to rain," she said.

There was nothing to do but move on. They walked for a good half hour along the road before the rain slowly began to stop. When they came to a picnic table in a small playground, they stopped and took out the chicken salad sandwiches, carrot sticks, and squares of chocolate that Gilbert had packed for them. They ate without speaking, and it was only when they were done that Jinny said, "Where do we go now, Manny?"

The truth was, Jinny had believed that if she went looking for Sullivan she would find him right away, the way she found him when they were playing hide-and-seek. It was only now that they had been out for a few hours that she realized it would not be as easy as she had imagined. They would not simply see him standing on a street corner or sitting on the curb having an ice cream. Finding him was going to be much harder than that.

Manny, of course, knew that finding Sullivan would be difficult. In fact, he knew that it was probably impossible. Despite what he had told the residents of the Stardust Home, he did not absolutely believe that Sullivan was alive. Manny had not really agreed to go looking in order to find Sullivan. He had agreed because he thought that Jinny *needed* to go looking. That she would never get over the loss of her brother if she didn't look. He was doing this for Jinny, not Sullivan.

But since they were looking, they might as well try their best. Manny said, "I'd like you to show me the spot where you and Sullivan watched that performance. That medicine show, as you called it. Maybe we'll learn something. Do you know where it was?"

"Runny Cold's Field," she said.

"Pardon?"

"That's what Sullivan called the place. Runny Cold's Field."

"Do you think you can find it?"

Jinny looked around. "Not from here," she said. "But if you take us to the store, the one where Sullivan and I go for candy, I think I can find it from there."

"All right, then." Manny got up, slinging his pack back on. He banged his cane on the ground, trying to show some enthusiasm that might raise Jinny's spirits as well as his own. "Let's go."

Jinny slung on her own backpack and banged her own cane, making it squeak. "Forward march!" she said, and began marching like a soldier.

"It's the other way, Jinny," Manny said.

"Backwards march!" she cried, doing just that.

By the time they reached the store, it was late afternoon. Both Manny's and Jinny's feet hurt from walking, but neither of them complained. They went on, past one farm and the next, past the stream and the billboard for condominiums. "Down there," Jinny said, pointing to the line of trees.

"Ah," Manny said. "You don't mean Runny Cold's Field. You mean *Reingold's* Field."

"That's what I said."

They used their canes as they moved down the slope. "It was right here," Jinny said. Manny looked at the ground. The dry grass was pressed flat here and there, but it was impossible to tell from what. There was an indentation that might have been from a wagon wheel, but then again it might have been from a million other things. Manny looked up and surveyed the area. He didn't see anything that might help them.

Jinny used her cane to search through the grass and the few low bushes nearby. The place brought back vivid memories of the two evenings — the strange music, the crowd, Sullivan's excitement as she clutched his hand. She pushed aside a clump of longer grass and saw something, a bit of paper, lying there. She picked it up and scrutinized it. Although she knew her letters, she still couldn't read. But she *did* recognize it.

"Manny, look," she said.

He came over and peered at the paper. "It's just a torn scrap," he said. "Most of it's missing. I can make out a few words. *Show.* And *Wonder.* And *Snoot.* And *Drops.* But what does it mean?"

"It's the flyer from the medicine show. Like the one we found. Snoot is the name of one of the dogs — I remember that. And drops, that's what the man was selling, little bottles of drops."

"Well, I'll be," Manny exclaimed. "Just like you said, Jinny. And if I know Sullivan, he would have wanted to see it again. Also like you said. This is indeed something. This is a start."

"Woohoo!" Jinny shouted, banging her squeaker cane on the ground. "Now what do we do?" she asked.

Manny looked at the sky. "The sun's going down. We can try one more thing. And then we'll have to find a place to stay for the night."

❋

They started walking again, but it was some time before they came to the next farm. It was not abandoned, or about to be turned into condominiums, but a real working farm, with fields of hay and cows being herded into the barn for the evening milking. Manny and Jinny watched from the fence, Manny saying that the farmer would be too busy to talk to them right now. So they waited until he came out of the barn again and walked to the house and took off his rubber boots and went inside. Then they went around to the gate and down the front path. It was an old red-brick house with painted wooden gables but also a satellite TV dish attached to the roof. Manny knocked on the front door and they waited until a woman in an apron appeared.

"I'm sorry, but we don't want to buy anything today."

"Oh, we don't wish to sell you anything at all," Manny said, taking off his hat.

"Or religion, either," the woman said. "We've got our own."

"No, no. We're looking for a boy, a family member who is lost. We're just wondering if by any chance you saw this."

Manny held out the scrap of paper. It only had the three words on it, but the woman's face changed, as if she recognized it. "Yes, we went to see them," she said. "You say a boy is lost? How awful. Let me call my husband. He was there, too."

Her husband, the man who had taken in the cows, was very big. He almost filled the entire front door, with his wife edged in beside him.

"These people are asking about the wagon show that came by."

"Yes, we saw it," the man confirmed. "Good, old-fashioned entertainment. A lot better than anything on television, even with all those new channels."

"By any chance did you see a boy there? About this high. Sandy hair. With a backpack."

"Not that I recall. But there was a good crowd, and I was watching the stage. What about you, Ellen?"

"I'm afraid I don't recall, either."

"Do you have any idea where they were going next?"

"No, I don't," the man said. "They were gone when I went by the field the next morning."

"I saw them leave," the woman said. "In the night. I couldn't sleep and I was in the kitchen having a cup of tea. I saw the wagon go by. It passed the house heading west. That way. And then it turned north at the tree stump there. There's a road going off, but you can't see it from here."

"That's a big help," Manny said. "We won't bother you anymore. Thank you."

But Jinny said, "Something sure smells goody-good in there."

The woman looked at her a moment. "Supper's almost ready. Are you hungry?"

"Starving," Jinny said.

"Then you'd better come in and join us. Is this boy related to you, young lady?"

"He's my brother. We're going to find him."

"I bet you are. And where you staying tonight?"

"Oh, probably under a barrel somewhere."

The man said, "We've got a guest room with two beds. You're welcome to it."

"That is very, very kind of you," Manny said. "We accept gladly. Perhaps over dinner you might describe the show that you saw. The acts, what the people looked like."

"Sure," agreed the man. "You think your boy ran off and joined them?"

"We don't know what to think." Manny shook his head.

"A good supper and a night's sleep are bound to help," said the woman, ushering them in. "I'll just put two more plates on the table."

19

HOW TO CLIMB AN INVISIBLE LADDER

SULLIVAN awoke to a changed landscape. The caravan was set up against a rise of hills, behind which rose even higher hills that were bare rock along their upper ridges. Small wildflowers grew, yellow and blue and white. The water from the nearby stream was cool and clear. Stumbling into the light and the fresh air, still groggy from sleep, Sullivan had felt with a pang how they were moving farther and farther away from Beanfield. Farther away from his family, from the Stardust Home, from anyone who knew him.

Now he stood on the dry ground covered in scraggly grass with his juggling equipment placed around him. He waited for Mistress Melville to come out of the caravan and tell him what his personality was going to be. But Mistress was taking her time. Clarence came around from behind the caravan, Snit and Snoot trotting behind him. He sauntered over to Sullivan, whistling, his hands in his pockets.

"I guess you don't have any reason to be nervous," Sullivan said.

"Well, I am. I've put a lot into your act. Actually, I always whistle when I'm nervous. But the Black Death has a good eye for talent and how to use it."

At that moment, Mistress Melville emerged from the caravan, and Clarence stopped talking. She wore a black bathrobe and black slippers and even a black hairnet. She walked directly over to them, looked sourly at Sullivan, and said, "You're the *accidental juggler.*"

"Accidental? What do you mean?"

"It means that you don't intend to juggle things. You're just an ordinary kid. With no special talent at all. Juggling just happens to you, by accident. Here's an example. You're walking across the stage, perhaps whistling in that annoying way that this little dog-keeper has. Walking down the street without a care in the world. You look down and notice three balls on the ground."

"How did they get there?"

Mistress Melville shook her head impatiently. "It doesn't matter how they got there. They just *are* there. So you pick up a ball and look at it. Then you pick up the other two. You shrug and pretend to throw them away but instead they come back down to you. Surprised, you catch them and throw them again. The whole time you're juggling—walking around, suddenly doing an under-the-leg move—you're totally surprised. Sometimes you're delighted by it—I mean, really amazed. And then other times, such as when you suddenly speed up and the balls look like they're going out of control, you're shocked and even scared. You see, it's all by accident. The crowd will laugh, but they'll be on your side, too."

Sullivan frowned as he listened. He thought about the idea. "You thought of this because I look so ordinary. Because it seems like there's nothing special at all about me."

"I thought of it because I know the audience will *like* you. Now get to work."

She turned around and walked back to the caravan. Only when she was gone did Sullivan speak to Clarence. "Juggling is hard enough," Sullivan said. "But trying to make it look like an accident? That'll be even harder."

"That's true. It'll take really good balancing skills. And control of your body so that you don't give away the moves, don't prepare yourself as if you expect to be juggling. And you have to really act. But all good performers do. It's brilliant. It'll be great, you'll see. I know you can do it."

Sullivan looked down. He kicked at one of his juggling balls with the toe of his shoe. "Okay," he said. "I'll try."

"Excellent. Let's get started."

❈

Becoming the accidental juggler turned out to be even more difficult than Sullivan expected. Acting as if he didn't mean to juggle meant that he couldn't stand in his usual way. He had to juggle while half turned, or with one foot behind the other, or even as he walked, or leaned over backwards, or pretended to stumble. Not only did it look totally fake at first, but he kept dropping the balls or the rings or whatever he was using. It felt as if all the improvements in juggling that he had made in the last weeks had suddenly vanished.

And then there was the acting part. Looking surprised when he knew just what was coming. Or afraid. Or gleeful. Or confused. He was even worse at all of that. Clarence called in Esmeralda to help. Esmeralda, Clarence told him, had taken acting classes. Glad to be of assistance, she began a crash course in acting that very afternoon that lasted a whole week. She began with exercises, like trying to move one part of his body without moving any other part—his big toe, his stomach, his right ear. He had to pretend he was a creature from another planet and find a new way to move himself across the ground. Then he was an explorer trying to communicate with people who spoke a language he had never heard before. Then came miming—climbing an invisible ladder, baking an invisible cake, drinking an invisible glass of water. When Clarence chuckled at him, Sullivan emptied an invisible glass over his head.

After that came more involved improvisations, like having to stand before a firing squad or jump out of an airplane. It was strange and disconcerting work, and the only part that Sullivan enjoyed was getting to spend time with Esmeralda. She was remarkably patient, and unlike Clarence, she never laughed at him. "I know you can do it, Dex," she said quietly when he got discouraged. Then she would put her arm around his shoulder and whisper suggestions into his ear, her red hair brushing against his cheek. And when he did something well, she would jump up and give him a hug, making him blush. The only thing he didn't like was catching sight of Frederick pretending not to watch them.

In the mornings, Sullivan continued to practice his juggling. At night, he found it hard to sleep. He couldn't stop going through the routines in his mind, his hands twitching as if they were catching and throwing objects. And when he did finally fall asleep, he would have weird and vivid dreams about jumping out of airplanes or running through fire. He would wake with a start only to find that it was dark and the caravan was still rolling on.

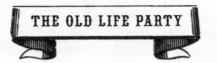

20

THE OLD LIFE PARTY

A TREMOR of excitement spread as they passed the news from one to another. Sullivan could see it move from Frederick to Esmeralda to Clarence, and at last it reached him, too. It had been four weeks since Sullivan arrived, and for the first time the Melvilles were going out. That meant that tonight the young performers were going to have an old life party, the first one in months.

Every so often, Clarence explained to Sullivan as he washed dishes in the basin while Clarence dried, instead of moving on right after dark, Master and Mistress Melville would go out. They would dress in their ghoulishly best clothes, lock the kids into the caravan, and set out for a night on the nearby town. What they did, nobody was exactly sure. A restaurant, a movie, or dancing, perhaps. All the kids knew was that they would not be back for hours.

And what was an old life party? Sullivan wanted to know. An old life party, Clarence said, was exactly what it sounded like. A party to remember the life each of them had before joining the medicine show. Family, friends, school — all that stuff. They would even use their real names, not the ones that the Melvilles had given them. They would say all the things that they could never say at any other time.

But a party wasn't a party without food, drink, decorations, and music. So each of them was assigned a task. Clarence was on dinner duty that day, so he had to snatch the food. Frederick would handle the drink — he was famous for his "mystery fruit punch." Esmeralda would make the decorations. That left Sullivan with the job of supplying the music.

"How can I get music?" Sullivan asked. "I mean, it's not like I can go out and hire a band. And we don't have an MP3 player or anything like that. It's impossible."

"Nothing is impossible," Clarence said with a shrug.

"That's right, ball boy," Frederick growled as he passed by. "You're not going to let us down, are you?"

"Don't you worry. I'll get us music," Sullivan spat back. He hated the way Frederick talked to him, as if he didn't belong there, as if he wasn't as good as the rest of them. He would show Frederick. He'd get music. Great music. He just didn't know how.

Over the course of the day, Clarence managed to hide a bag of carrots, a block of cheddar cheese, a half-jar of pickles and another of peanut butter, some crackers, a container of strawberries, and a bar of chocolate. "Just wait and see what I do with these!" he said happily.

For decorations, Esmeralda decided on an underwater theme. When the Melvilles weren't watching, she took some old newspapers, cut them into strips, and began to color them blue and green with sticks of stage makeup. Frederick, meanwhile, worked inside the caravan, mixing up his famous punch, the recipe for which he kept as secret as Master Melville's recipe for Hop-Hop Drops.

The only one who didn't know what to do was Sullivan. He thought of trying to swipe Mistress Melville's musical instruments — her drum, her banjo-ukulele, her kazoo. But Mistress was very fond of her instruments and spent a lot of time cleaning and polishing them. She didn't even let Master Melville touch them, and Sullivan didn't want to imagine what she would do if she found out he had. Besides, none of them could play. He thought of singing, only he could never remember the words to songs, and besides, he had a hard time keeping a tune. By late afternoon, when the others were starting to get ready for the evening performance, he still had nothing. He was going to let them down.

Sullivan was sitting on a tree stump feeling depressed when Master Melville came by, using a brush on his black top hat. "Why the long face, dear boy?" he asked. "You must make the best of it, whatever the circumstances. I learned that early in life."

"Yes, sir."

Master Melville crouched down. "Don't tell me. You've got something to do and you don't know how to do it. Something for a certain event."

Sullivan looked at Master Melville in surprise. He almost blurted out, *You know about the party?* but managed to stop himself. Maybe Master Melville suspected something and was trying to trick him.

"Do not worry, dear boy, I have no nefarious designs. Between you and me, I know about these little shindigs. Personally, I think it's good for you all to blow off a little steam. Get your feelings out. Mistress Melville, well, she might have a different attitude. But why worry her, eh? It's hardly important enough, I'd say. So if I find a little food missing, or something else is amiss, I take care of it myself. You see? I've got your best interests at heart. Now I wonder what your task is."

Sullivan hesitated. If this was a trick and he gave the party away, he would be betraying all of them. But something made him believe that Master Melville was being sincere. Maybe Sullivan could respond in a way that didn't incriminate them.

"It's always nice to have a little music," he ventured.

"Of course. What is a social occasion without the sweet strains of melody? I understand. But it is a tricky request to fulfill."

"It's impossible," said Sullivan, and then immediately realized that he had forgotten to be careful.

"Well, it just so happens that I have an old wind-up gramophone and a box of records. A little temperamental, but it works. Mistress and I sometimes listen on the road while the rest of you are all fast asleep."

"Yes, I've heard it," Sullivan said. "I thought I was dreaming."

"Mind you, it could use a good dusting. And since

you've got nothing to do, I don't see why I shouldn't put you to work."

"Put me to work," Sullivan said. "Please put me to work."

"I will, then. Dexter," he said in a louder voice, "I see you've got nothing useful to do. In that case, you can clean and polish my gramophone. And the records, too. I expect to have it all back first thing tomorrow morning. Or there will be trouble. Do you understand?"

"Yes, Master Melville. Thank you."

"Thank me? For giving you extra work? You are a strange boy. Now come along and I'll give it to you. And be careful with it! If you damage it there will be severe consequences, I promise you that."

Master Melville turned on his heel and strode toward the caravan. "Yes!" Sullivan whispered under his breath, and he ran to catch up.

❈

The show that night could not have been called anyone's best performance, Sullivan thought. Everyone was too excited about the old life party to concentrate properly. Frederick dropped a handful of cards that were hidden behind his hand. Napoleon the chess-playing automaton lost to a boy in high school. Master

Melville hissed at them as they came offstage, but he didn't seem to mean it. The truth was that he, too, must have been looking forward to the evening out with Mistress, because his pitches for the Hop-Hop Drops lacked their usual spark.

When the show was over and the last bottle sold, everyone rushed to clean up. The stage became the side of the caravan again, the props got put away, the horse was given his nightly oats. "Hurry up and get to bed!" grumbled Master Melville unnecessarily, for they were all in their pajamas and tucked into their bunks in record time.

The person who *did* take a long time was Mistress Melville. Sullivan could hear her husband pleading for her to hurry. But at last Sullivan heard her come out of the Melvilles' side of the caravan and step down. A moment later the back door swung open, and in the light cast from a small lamp held in Master Melville's hand, Sullivan could see both of them peering in, framed in the doorway. Mistress wore a tight black bodice, cut low and with a small diamond pendant dangling against her pale skin. Her lips were painted blood red, and dark makeup lined her eyes. Her black leather gloves went up to her elbows.

"Hurry up, Monty," said Mistress. "Lock them in."

"You get up on the horse, love of my life. I'll be there in a moment."

"You will if you know what's good for you."

She moved away. Master Melville took his ring of keys from his pocket. "Night-night, dear boys and dear girl," he said. When he smiled, a gold tooth glinted. "Do enjoy yourselves." He shut the door and fastened the padlock.

Silence. No one so much as stirred. Sullivan lay in the dark, listening to the fading clip-clop of Soggy Biscuit's hooves. They waited, but for what?

A match flared and then a candle was lit.

"All right, everyone," said Clarence. "It's party time!"

They threw off their covers. Clarence lit more candles standing in blue or yellow or red jars, casting colored streaks of light. Esmeralda pulled at paper tabs here and there, releasing her decorations, which dangled from the ceiling. Frederick slid the big bowl of his mystery punch from under his bunk, and Clarence brought out the trays of food. He had turned the various items he had snatched into hors d'oeuvres —cheese and pickle on crackers, carrot sticks spread with peanut butter, strawberries covered in chocolate.

Now it was Sullivan's turn. The gramophone was covered by an extra blanket at the end of his bed. He pulled it off to reveal the small oak box with a crank at one end and a flat, circular table and arm on top. From the foot of his bunk he drew out a brass horn, with a wide mouth that tapered down to a narrow end, which Sullivan attached to the box. It was a good thing that Master Melville had left instructions tucked inside the horn. From under the bed he produced a stack of small records in paper sleeves. He pulled one out, put it on the circular table, turned the crank, and lowered the arm. He looked up to see the others watching him as the scratchy, faraway sounds of a long-dead orchestra began to play. A woman sang:

> *I've been to Argentina*
> *And the Smoky Mountains too,*
> *I've seen the view of Naples*
> *But it means nothing without you . . .*

Clarence smiled. Swaying to the music, Frederick began scooping soup-spoons of punch into mugs. Esmeralda got up again, standing in the candlelight in her nightgown. She walked to Sullivan's bunk and said, "May I have this dance?"

"But I don't—"

Esmeralda pulled him up. She put one of his hands on her waist, held his other with her own, and began to waltz up the narrow aisle. Her touch was soft and warm, and she smelled like lemons.

"Divine," Esmeralda said. "It's too, too divine."

It was the best party Sullivan had ever been to. They ate and they drank and they danced and they laughed. Even Frederick. Sullivan finally heard, for the first time, what Clarence and Frederick and Esmeralda's real names were. And when someone, instead of calling him Dexter, said, "Care for another mug of punch, Sullivan?" or "Stop making me laugh, Sullivan!" he felt tears sting his eyes and he had to quickly wipe them away.

When finally they became tired from dancing and the lateness of the hour, they sat on their bunks and talked quietly by the light of a single remaining candle. They had heard all of the records many times, but it was that first song they liked best, and they asked Sullivan to put it on the gramophone again.

I've seen lions on safari
And the top of Katmandu,
I've drunk champagne in Paris
And thought only about you . . .

And when it was over and there was only the soft hissing sound of the needle on the cylinder going round and round, Clarence—whose real name was Matt—said, "I'll go first."

"First?" Sullivan asked.

But Clarence just went on. He said, "Pancakes. My dad made pancakes every Sunday morning. With blueberries, in the summer. And lots of maple syrup. He would sing opera in a really off-key voice while he flipped the pancakes in the pan. And my brothers and I would argue about who got the next one. When I close my eyes I can taste those sweet pancakes. And I can hear my dad singing."

The others raised their mugs of punch and drank, so Sullivan followed suit.

Esmeralda—whose real name was Louise, even though she didn't look at all like a Louise to Sullivan—said, "One time I had this nightmare. I was really little, only five or six. I dreamed that these ghosts in bowler hats and glasses were chasing me."

"Bowler hats aren't exactly scary," said Frederick. (In real life, he was Oscar.)

"Well, they were scary to me. I was screaming, but no sound came out of my mouth, and then they were about to grab me and I woke up. My parents let me keep a flashlight by my bed, and I turned it on and walked down the hall to their room. They were still up, watching an old black-and-white movie on TV. I still remember what it was called. *The Philadelphia Story.* They let me snuggle in between them and watch with them. Only I fell asleep before it was over."

Again, the kids raised their mugs and drank. "Sweet," Clarence said at last. "Very sweet. We know to skip Oscar, so it's Sullivan's turn."

"Why do we skip Frederick—I mean, Oscar?" Sullivan asked.

"Because he won't do it."

"That's right," said Frederick. "So go ahead."

"I don't know what to say," Sullivan said. "I haven't had time to think about it."

"You don't have to think," said Clarence. "Just tell us the first memory that comes to mind."

"Okay . . . I guess my birthday, two years ago. My little sister, Jinny, insisted on singing 'Happy Birthday' to me all by herself. Standing on a chair. Wearing a paper crown. Holding a fork. Only she used to get words wrong all the time—she still does, sometimes—and she sang, 'Hopping Bird Day to You.' It was so funny, but me and my mom and dad were trying not to laugh and hurt her feelings. And ever since then we've always sung 'Hopping Bird Day' on our birthdays."

There was a silence as they all drank their punch. Then Esmeralda said, "That was a good one."

"Yeah, really good," Clarence agreed.

And at that moment, they heard something. It was the squeak of a foot on the step up to the front bench of the caravan. Then came the sound of Soggy Biscuit being hitched to the caravan. The horse whinnied and a moment later the wheels began to turn.

"Party's over," said Frederick, yawning.

"Good night, everybody," said Esmeralda.

Clarence blew out the candle. Sullivan put away the gramophone and lay down in his bunk, pulling up the blanket. During the party he had been truly happy for the first time since being locked inside that trunk. But talking about his old life had brought it all back to him, so that the pain of homesickness, which had subsided to a dull throb, grew sharp again. He missed his sister, Jinny. He missed his mother and his father. He missed Manny Morgenstern and the Stardust Home. But at the same time, he realized that he had never had such close friends as he did now in the caravan. It was a strange thought, but it was true.

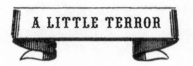

21

A LITTLE TERROR

$\mathcal{J}$UST as a book does not truly come alive until someone opens it and begins to read, so a performer needs an audience. A few days after the old life party, they found themselves camped beside an abandoned miniature golf course. It still had its worn plastic grass, a little bridge, even a windmill, although two of the wooden blades were broken off. There were some clubs and balls lying about and Frederick and Esmeralda immediately began to play. Master Melville didn't seem very happy to see the golf course and cursed under his breath. Sullivan had noticed that he never liked anything that looked as if it had been built in the last fifty years.

The land around the course was flat and boring. Sullivan watched Esmeralda miss the ball, laugh at herself, and then ask Frederick to show her how to hold the club. "Let's play too," he said to Clarence.

"Listen, Dex," Clarence pronounced slowly, ignoring his suggestion. "I think you're ready."

"Ready? To go on stage, you mean?"

"Not quite, Dex. You're ready to show the act to the Monsters Melville. I'll go and tell them."

"This moment? Without warning me? Without practice?"

"You've been practicing for days. No point in giving you time to get nervous."

"It doesn't take me any time to get nervous. I can get nervous in a second. I'm nervous right now. My knees are shaking."

"Good. You don't want *not* to be nervous, either. I'll be back."

With a sinking stomach, Sullivan watched Clarence approach Master Melville, who listened to him, nodded, and walked over to his wife. Then Melville shooed the other performers — except for Clarence, the "director"—into the caravan. A moment later, Master and Mistress were walking toward Sullivan, Clarence at their side.

Sullivan closed his eyes and wished that he would disappear. It was a childish wish, he knew, but he wished it anyway.

He opened his eyes. And saw them standing in front of him.

"Don't dawdle," said Mistress peevishly, not even looking at him. Sullivan always had the impression that it annoyed her immensely to have to acknowledge his existence. "I don't want to stand here all day."

"Yes, get on with it," said Master Melville.

"Right," said Clarence. "I'll just set things up on the grass as if it were the stage. Come on, Sullivan, go to your starting place offstage."

Sullivan watched as Clarence went to get the balls and other objects and arranged them on the ground.

"Monty," said Mistress. "Fetch me a chair."

"Of course, my petunia, how thoughtless of me."

They waited as he hurried to the side of the caravan, picked up a folding chair, and brought it back. Mistress Melville looked down at it a moment, as if it might not be clean enough, and finally sat. Sullivan looked with a surge of panic over to Clarence, who nodded, signaling him to begin.

And so he began. He wished Mistress Melville were playing her instruments—the afternoon felt absolutely silent as he pretended to wander onto the stage and then notice the balls lying there. He picked one up, another, then acted as if he meant to throw one away but found himself catching it again. He kicked the third ball on the ground, actually lifting it up into the air. And then he was juggling all three, his throwing a little off so that he had to lunge to catch a stray ball here and there, but fortunately, that could be seen as an intentional part of his "accidental" juggling routine.

The rest of the act went well enough, though he felt as if he were in a dream. He forgot most of what Esmeralda had taught him about acting. At last he performed his final spin, caught the toaster, rubber boot, and china pig, and took a bow.

There was a moment of total silence. And then Master Melville stood up and began to clap vigorously. "Bravo!" he said. "Well done. An excellent routine. Amusing and original. The boy comes off as very likable. I take my hat off to both of you."

Sullivan turned to Clarence, who looked visibly relieved. Clarence looked back at him and grinned.

Mistress stood up. "Drop the clubs," she said.

"What's that, my beloved?"

"The clubs. They aren't different enough. They bored me to tears. Get rid of them."

"Of course, you're right as always. Once more your keen artistic eye proves itself. But without them, the act will be too short. The boy needs something else instead."

Mistress Melville shook her head with impatience. "Torches," she said flatly.

Sullivan heard the word with alarm. "Torches? You mean, as in *fire?*"

"Of course I mean flaming torches. What good would they be if they weren't on fire? The audience always enjoys feeling a little terror on behalf of the performer. The boy can make his debut in three days."

"That might be a little soon, my sweet —"

"It isn't soon enough, in my opinion. It's about time he started to earn his keep."

At that she stood up, knocked over the chair, and walked away. Master Melville picked it up and hurried after her. Immediately, Sullivan went over to Clarence.

"Torches? There's no way I'm juggling fire."

"It's not that hard," Clarence said. "It's just like clubs. You just have to make sure you don't grab the wrong end."

❈

Sullivan did not know where Master Melville found three juggling torches, but the next day they were on Sullivan's bunk. They had obviously been used before, the ends scorched from having been lit many times. The handles were just like those on his clubs, but the rest looked kind of like a giant match, with a bulb at the end. Clarence instructed Sullivan to juggle them unlit first, to get used to their weight and feel. Luckily, they felt a lot like his clubs, and it took him only a half hour or so to feel comfortable with them. Then Clarence showed Sullivan how to dip the bulb end of each torch into a bowl of liquid fuel, carefully shaking off the excess.

"That fuel's dangerous stuff, so be careful. Now go ahead and light one."

"*You* light one," Sullivan said. "I don't want to."

"Well, I don't want to, either. You're the juggler."

Sullivan gave Clarence a dark look and picked up the box of matches. He struck one and then held it to the bulb of a torch. Immediately it whooshed into flame, causing him to hold it as far away from himself as he could. When the fire had calmed a little, he touched the first torch to the second and third, and they, too, whooshed into flame, flickering and hissing.

"Remember," Clarence said. "Stay in control. Don't

try any moves that you can't do perfectly every time. And don't worry. I've got a bucket of water to throw on you just in case."

"Very comforting," Sullivan said. He placed his feet, held the flaming torches, breathed in and out, and began.

He was juggling fire.

He could feel the heat from the torches on his face as they passed up or down. Slowly, Sullivan relaxed, falling into the rhythm of the routine.

"Hey, this is kind of fun," he said.

"Not too fun, I hope," Clarence replied. "Don't forget that you're playing with fire. *Really* playing with fire, I mean."

For two whole days, Sullivan practiced with the torches. He practiced lighting them, juggling them, and extinguishing them, over and over. If he forgot some safety measure, such as moving away from the bowl of fuel before starting to juggle, Clarence would stop him.

"Remember how you used to balance a club on your nose?" Clarence asked. "Well, a torch is really just a club."

"This is where I draw the line," Sullivan said. "I am *not* balancing a torch on my nose."

"It's your choice."

"You know I'm going to try, don't you?"

"Yes, I do," Clarence said, and smiled.

❃

On the day of his first performance on stage, Sullivan practiced all morning, running through the act over and over. Badly. He dropped balls, he dropped the toaster, he even let a flaming torch land between his feet and jumped away, yelping. Then it was time for lunch. After lunch, he went into the bushes and threw up.

Esmeralda brought him a cup of water and a towel. "It's normal," she said, putting her hand on his arm and walking him back toward the caravan. "On the day of my first show, I fainted three times."

"Maybe ball boy isn't meant for the stage," said Frederick, who was leaning against the caravan and spreading a deck of cards along the length of his arm. With a flick of his shoulder he made the first card turn over, flipping all the rest.

"He'll do great," Clarence said, patting Sullivan on the back. But Sullivan wasn't so sure. What if Clarence and Esmeralda were wrong and Frederick was right? What if he didn't have what it takes? The talent, the courage, the ambition—whatever it was that made a person a real performer. His stomach churned.

He ran for the bushes again.

Soon it was time to prepare for the performance. He and Clarence lowered the side of the caravan to make the stage, and put up the curtain and the wings. Frederick ironed his tuxedo and loaded the pockets. Esmeralda did her stretching exercises.

Clarence had to sew up a tear in Napoleon's jacket. "Some little kid poked it with a stick yesterday while I was in the middle of the game," he said. "But the worst thing is that it's just getting too tight in there. I might not be very big, but I'm still growing. I can hardly breathe."

"What's going to happen when you're too big to fit in it?" Sullivan asked.

"Good question."

Just then Frederick called out, "I see the first mark!"

Sullivan shaded his eyes against the sinking sun. The stage was set up in a meadow strewn with tiny white flowers. In the distance was a fence with a stile —a set of steps on either side for climbing over. He saw four figures wait their turn to go over the stile. As they began to cross the meadow, more people approached.

The other performers scrambled to their places. Sullivan shook himself, whispered "Help me" under his breath, and hurried to the wing.

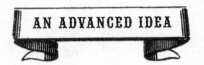

AN ADVANCED IDEA

MANNY Morgenstern used his cane to open the door of the telephone booth. He stepped out to where Jinny was waiting for him. She was sitting on the grass at the side of the road, hunting for four-leaf clovers. They needed luck, and finding one was the best way she could think of to get some.

The eighty-one-year-old man and the six-year-old girl had been on the road now for over four weeks. In that time, spring had turned into early summer. Manny had promised Jinny's parents that they would come home after two weeks, but Gilbert and Loretta had reluctantly agreed to let them keep looking for a while longer. "I don't think Jinny is ready to give up," Manny had told them on the phone. "She might just run away again." But still they had found nothing. Oh, there was a rumor here and there of a wagon passing in the night, or somebody hearing from a cousin about somebody else seeing an act on a little stage — vague whispers that sent them in a westerly direction — but that was all. They had slept in cheap and not very clean motels, in rented rooms, in dusty attics and damp basements, and a few times in the homes of kindly people who fed them sorely needed home-cooked meals. Every day, Manny had given Jinny a reading and an arithmetic lesson.

The telephone booth was outside a general store called Muckricker's Feed and Supply. The store was on the edge of a town called Perlitsky, population three hundred and seventy-five. Manny had just phoned Gilbert and Loretta, letting them know that he and Jinny were all right and not to worry. Still, Jinny's parents both said that it might be time to come home. In truth, Manny wasn't so sure they were all right. They were tired, they both had blisters on their feet, Jinny was having nightmares and missed her parents, and Manny was having chest pains. After hanging up, he had phoned the police department and had spoken to Officer Spoonitch. "It's official," the police officer had said with regret in his voice. "Drowning, no body recovered. The Mintz case is closed. I'm sorry."

Jinny didn't find any four-leaf clovers. Finally, she pulled a three-leaf clover out of the ground and split one of the leaves in two. If she couldn't find luck, she decided, then she would have to make it. She saw Manny emerge from the booth and asked, "What did the police say? Are they going to send a bunch of heli-crappers?"

"No helicopters right now," Manny said. He looked through the window of the general store and saw that it had an old-fashioned counter with stools and a soda fountain. "I think we could use a pick-me-up," he added. "How about we go inside and have ourselves a couple of vanilla milk shakes?"

"I like strawberry," Jinny said.

"Strawberry it is."

So they went through the door and up to the counter, and Manny helped Jinny get up onto a stool. The man behind the cash register came over, put on an apron, and said, "What can I get for you?" He was thin and had a crooked nose and a comb-over, his hair long on one side and so he could sweep it over to cover his bald spot.

"One vanilla milk shake and one strawberry," Manny said.

"Coming right up."

While the man made their milk shakes, they looked around. The store had shovels and rakes hanging from the ceiling, pots and pans on the shelves, batteries, snow boots, and just about anything else you could think of. By the counter was a bulletin board where people had posted notices. There were two for lost dogs, one with a pasted-on photograph of a tractor that was for sale, another offering yoga classes. Jinny sounded out some of the words that she could see from her perch on the stool.

The man put their milk shakes on the counter. They were in tall, cold glasses, with long spoons.

"Delicious," said Jinny.

"Mmm," agreed Manny.

For a while they slurped in silence. Then Jinny said, "Manny, remember I told you about the medicine show?"

"Of course," said Manny.

"And that the people on stage were kids? The boy who did magic and the smaller boy with the dogs and the girl on the piperope — I mean, tightrope."

"Sure, I remember."

"Where do you think they came from?"

"I don't know."

"They must have moms and dads too, right? And Mannys."

"I'm not sure about the Manny part, but sure, they must have parents." Manny nodded slowly. "I understand what you're saying. Maybe those kids disappeared, too. And their parents are also trying to find them. Or have given up. But those parents are out there and maybe they know something. So we should find them. That's brilliant, Jinny."

Jinny smiled. "I know," she said. "I'm very advanced for my age."

❋

At many schools these days the office is a hive of activity. Students come in to make announcements over the PA system, to help the secretaries, to plan assemblies and special events. They feel at home, as if the office, like the rest of the school, truly belongs to them.

But in some schools that have not changed with the times, the office is still a place where students go for only one of three reasons. They need a late slip, they need to leave early, or they are in trouble. Beanfield Middle School was, unfortunately, one of these schools.

Norval Simick had never gone to the office before.

And he had never wanted to. But now he sat on the hard wooden bench that faced the counter behind which the secretaries worked. He felt his knees shaking.

Beside him sat Samuel Patinsky. Samuel *had* been in the office before—nine times, in fact. Each time he'd been sent there by a teacher for not doing his homework, or for throwing pencils, or (in one instance) for dangling the guts of a dead frog in a girl's face during science class. But he'd never before gone to the office *voluntarily*, and he was more nervous this time than he had ever been.

Norval and Samuel had come prepared. In Norval's hand was a folder filled with twelve pages describing their plans for a Sullivan Mintz Celebration Day. The two of them had worked together, after school and on weekends, for hours.

One of the secretaries leaned over the counter. "All right, you two," she said without smiling. "Mr. Washburb will see you in his office. Hurry up now— he's a busy man."

Norval nodded his determination at Samuel, and Samuel nodded back. Then they got up and marched single file into the principal's office. Norval entered first and reached out to shake Principal Washburb's hand. The principal looked surprised, but he half rose out of his chair and took Norval's hand in his own. Samuel did the same. Then they sat down.

"Well, well," said Mr. Washburb. "It's been a while since you've had to come to my office, Samuel. As for you, ah, Norval," he said, looking down at a sheet of paper, "I'm sorry to see you getting into trouble for the first time. Now tell me what you two did to get sent here. Lit a stink bomb? Wrote something nasty on the board?"

"No, you've got it wrong," Norval said, leaning forward. "Nobody sent us. We came on our own."

"That's right," Samuel said.

"I see. You want to turn yourselves in."

"No, that's not it, either," Norval insisted. "We're not in trouble. We haven't done anything wrong. We're here with a proposal."

"That's right, a proposal," Samuel concurred.

"Hmm, I see. Rather unusual. All right then, what is it that you propose?"

Norval motioned to his partner, and Samuel took a deep breath. "We'd like to hold a Sullivan Mintz Celebration Day."

"The boy who drowned?"

"Yes," Norval said. "We don't want him to be forgotten. He went to this school. He belonged here, or at least he should have. We want to hold a special day —"

"A special day, you say? You mean, a whole day?"

"That's right, Principal Washburb. A day remembering and celebrating Sullivan. Here, it's all laid out in these plans." Norval slid the folder across the desk.

Principal Washburb used two fingers to open the folder. "Hmm," he muttered as he looked over the top of his glasses. He scanned the first page, turned it, looked at the next, and so went through all twelve pages. "You've done a lot of work. A great deal of work." He closed the folder and picked it up. Then he opened a desk drawer, dropped the folder into it, closed the drawer, and locked it with a little key. "I don't know what you're trying to pull here."

"Pardon me?" Norval said.

"Obviously this is some kind of stunt to humiliate me and the school. So let me assure you, there will be no Solomon Mint Celebration Day."

"That's *Sullivan Mintz*," said Samuel. "And why not?"

"Remembering a boy who died? Even if you weren't trying to pull something, how is that going to help anybody learn their times tables or know who won the War of 1812? It's just going to upset the student body. Make people depressed. Besides, I know for a fact that almost nobody in this school even remembers him. Listen, you two. It's almost summer vacation. The school year will be over soon. By next fall this unfortunate incident will have completely vanished from the students' thoughts, which is just the way I want it. Now the two of you had better get back to your class before I find another reason for you to be here."

And before they knew it, Norval and Samuel were back in the hallway, walking slowly to class. "We should have known Washburb would say no," Samuel said. "He doesn't care. Nobody does."

"No, that isn't true. People do care. Or, they will."

"Come on, Norval, it's over. Let's just forget about it."

Norval grabbed Samuel's hefty arm and pulled him to a stop. "No, we're not going to forget about it. This is about Sullivan. It's *for* Sullivan."

"What are we going to do?" Samuel asked.

"We're going to have Sullivan Mintz Celebration Day, that's what. With or without permission. And soon."

Frowning, Samuel looked down at Norval. But slowly his frown turned into a grin. "Oh, yeah," he said. "I like the sound of that."

❉

Gilbert and Loretta agreed to let Manny and Jinny stay out for one more week. With their help, Manny placed a classified advertisement in hundreds of small newspapers across the country.

HAVE YOU LOST YOUR CHILD?

Has your son or daughter gone missing? Did he or she like to do magic tricks, or walk on a tightrope, or perform in some other way? Did he or she vanish without a trace? If so, please contact Gilbert and Loretta Mintz at the Stardust Home for Old People in the town of Beanfield.

For the next few days, Manny and Jinny continued to look for Sullivan. They showed his picture to people in stores and on the sidewalks. They asked if anyone had seen an old-fashioned wagon or heard about a medicine show.

Then one afternoon nearly a week after the advertisements went out, as the pair walked down the main street of another small town, Manny said, "Now, listen, Jinny. You have to understand that this ad might not bring us any closer to finding Sullivan. I guess there are a lot of missing children out there because your parents have been overwhelmed with responses. But so far, none of the people's stories have matched the pattern of Sullivan's disappearance. This idea might just lead us to another dead end."

"But we still might hear from somebody whose

story does match," Jinny said. "We're not going to give up yet, right?"

"No, of course not," Manny replied, a little sadly. "And it's still early. We don't have to give up hope."

But the truth was that Manny didn't have much hope left. They had been looking for a long time, without success, and they were worn out. Jinny needed to be with her parents. She needed to go back to school and play with other kids. At this point, the most he hoped for was a way to help Jinny find some sense of peace and acceptance before they returned to Beanfield and got on with their lives.

"You know," Manny said, "just because we can't find Sullivan, doesn't mean he isn't out there somewhere. Maybe he's fine. Maybe he's thinking about us, too. Of course, there's still a chance your parents will uncover some new clues because of our advertisement. Then the case could be reopened, and the police will take over. Either way, the time has come for us to go home, Jinny. We've made some progress and done our best, and I have a feeling that, wherever he is, Sullivan would be just so proud of you."

Jinny didn't say anything, but for the first time she didn't argue against going home. Instead, she took Manny's hand and they kept walking.

THE FIRST TIME

🅣HE first time for anything can have a powerful significance. A child's first step, a teenager's first kiss, an adult's first day at work. It's true that people don't remember most of their firsts, and some of them they'd rather forget. But as Sullivan stood there in the wings behind the curtain and peeked out, he knew that this was a night he would never forget as long as he lived. What it would mean to him — that, he couldn't know.

Sullivan saw a family of four approaching the stage. Then a couple of teenagers, some men by themselves with their hands in their pockets, a young man with a young woman holding a bunch of wildflowers. Then more families, kids jostling against one another on the grass, until there were thirty or forty in the crowd pressed in front of the caravan stage.

The lanterns on either side cast their light onto the faces waiting for the show to begin. Sullivan peeked out again, although he had been told more than once by Frederick that it was unprofessional. He could feel his whole body trembling. His breathing was quick and shallow. Master Melville had scheduled him last so that he could make a point of introducing him for the first time ever, which meant that Sullivan had to watch everyone else before he could get his own act over with. If he could have thought of some way to get out of going on at all, he would have done it. But he had stopped throwing up, and even though he had felt faint once or twice, he hadn't managed to get himself to black out.

And then there was that small part of him that *wanted* to go on. That wanted to see if he really could perform in front of an audience. That wanted to see if they *liked* him.

Esmeralda came up and kissed him on the cheek. "You'll be great, I know you will. Try to relax and enjoy yourself."

"Enjoy myself?"

"That's right, Dex," said Clarence, coming up behind him. "The audience can't enjoy your act unless you do. Just keep focused. And remember, a mistake isn't the end of the world. There isn't any such thing as perfection. Just smile and keep going."

Sullivan had been warned about perfection before, but at the moment he couldn't remember when. He felt a push against his shoulder. It was Frederick. "Don't block my way when I have to go on, ball boy. Try not to be too big a disaster. I don't want to have to mop up after you."

"After me?"

"Why do you always repeat what I say? Master Melville told me that if you bomb I have to hurry onto the stage and do some more tricks so they don't go away without buying any Hop-Hop Drops. So *try* not to stink, all right?"

Oh, great, thought Sullivan. As if he wasn't feeling enough pressure. And then there was Mistress Melville, who didn't say anything but glared at him from behind her drum and washboard and banjo-ukulele as she took her position beside the stage. It felt as if her dark eyes bored right through him.

Then she began to play her introductory tune, beginning with a low rumble on the drum, then a hypnotic rhythm on the washboard, then an accompanying strum on the banjo-ukulele, and finally the melody on the kazoo. From the opposite wing, Master Melville entered the stage with a welcoming sweep of his arms. He smiled and laughed and joked and winked, making friends with the audience, and then introduced Frederick, who, once again, shoved Sullivan's shoulder as he went by.

Maybe there wasn't such a thing as perfection, Sullivan thought, but Frederick sure looked as if he performed every illusion flawlessly. He received loud applause from the crowd. Next came the chess-playing Napoleon, who did battle against a man who said that he was a high school mathematics teacher. The game went back and forth, one moment the man winning a bishop, the next Napoleon knocking over a knight. But at last Napoleon was victorious, and as his bells rang, and his wooden hand pinched his three-corner hat and raised it up and down, the crowd whooped.

Paralyzed by the thought of having to go on soon, Sullivan momentarily forgot his job following the automaton's performance. He had to run to the back of the stage and pull out Clarence, who was half fainting from lack of oxygen. "I can't . . . I can't do it anymore," he said. "I've grown too much." But he had no time to recover, only to wipe the sweat from his face and prepare Snit and Snoot for their act.

And despite his exhaustion, Clarence's dog act went wonderfully. The audience laughed from beginning to end. Was everyone especially brilliant and talented tonight, or did it just seem so to Sullivan? He felt his heart race even faster as Esmeralda performed on the tightrope, knowing that he was next. He didn't know how someone could be so lovely and graceful *and* funny *and* silly all at the same time, but somehow Esmeralda was.

As soon as the curtain closed, Frederick took down the tightrope and Clarence began to set out Sullivan's juggling props. Master Melville came out in front of the curtain.

"Ladies and gentlemen, what a positive smorgasbord of talent you have seen tonight. Young people at the pinnacle of their peculiar art forms. And in a moment I will have the honor of offering you the effective relief of Master Melville's Hop-Hop Drops at only ten dollars a bottle. But our show is not over, no sir. First, we have for you an extraordinarily special event. An artist so fresh, so young, so inexperienced that he has never before graced this or any other stage. But an artist who I sincerely believe is destined for the greatest triumphs. You, ladies and gentlemen, are witnessing the birth of a star. May I present, for the first time ever, *Dexter, the Accidental Juggler!*"

Sullivan didn't move. He knew that he was supposed to; he just couldn't get his feet to work. He felt a hard shove against his back—he knew without thinking that it was Frederick—and found himself stumbling onto the stage. A few chuckles came from the crowd. He regained his composure and did what he had practiced, whistling as he pretended to walk down a street. He passed the three balls, kept going, stopped, backed up. He looked at the balls. Then he looked at the audience.

The audience laughed.

He could see only the first row of upturned faces in the lantern light, but the laughter made him a little less nervous. He picked up one ball, felt its weight in his hand. Suddenly it was in the air and he had to reach out and—yes—snatch it. He smiled at the audience, as if to say, *I sure never expected to catch it.* He picked up the second ball, felt the two in his hands, threw one into the air, and then, looking shocked, threw the other. A moment later, he had kicked up the third.

He did not drop a ball, did not even fear that he would. And when the audience gasped with delight or laughed or held their breath, it felt completely natural to him, as if their reaction was the only thing that had ever been missing. He finished the ball routine by tossing them so high that they flew right over the caravan (where Esmeralda would gather them up).

The rings came next. And after them the toaster, the rubber boot, and the china pig. They had been set on a little table with a sign saying GARAGE SALE leaning against it. He picked up the boot first, then looked around for the other but couldn't find it. So he picked up the toaster and pushed down the lever. He put the boot and the toaster under one arm, and picked up the china pig. He shook it near his ear to hear if there was any money inside. Nope. He shrugged and was about to put the pig down again when he tripped . . . and threw the pig, the toaster, and the boot up in the air.

And kept throwing them. A look of confusion on his face, he walked about the stage. He tried to put the objects down, but somehow they kept going up. He spun around and still caught them. He threw them higher and higher, trying to get rid of them, and then —*bang, bang, bang*—one after another they came down into his arms as he fell to the ground.

And got up smiling.

All that was left were the flaming torches. Clarence had directed this part of the act as a little lesson in the danger of playing with matches. Recovering from his encounter with the household objects, Sullivan next found a box of matches on the ground. He picked them up, looked from side to side to make sure nobody was watching him, and then lit one. He gleefully held up its little flame.

Then he noticed the three torches on the ground. If lighting a match was fun, surely lighting one of these big things would be even more fun! With a big smile on his face, Sullivan lit a torch.

Whoosh!

He reeled back from the sudden flame. By accident, he touched it to the other two torches — *whoosh* and *whoosh* again! This was a lot of fire. The expression on Sullivan's face was more than worried. He had to get rid of them somehow. How about throwing them away? But what comes up must come down . . . and a moment later, he was juggling fire.

Because he looked terrified, the audience feared for him. But Sullivan had practiced so much that he knew he would not drop a torch, just as he hadn't dropped anything else in the act, unless it was intentional. And the audience, despite its fear, somehow knew that the boy with the torches would not fail. Not even when he balanced one on his nose. And when at last he threw them all into the air, picked up a bucket of water, and caught each one in it, sizzling as it went out, they whistled and cheered and stamped their feet.

Sullivan put down the bucket. And ran off the stage.

Master Melville caught him in the wing. "Back, dear boy, back you go to take your bow. Don't you hear them? You're a hit! They want to applaud you again! Go!"

And so he walked out and, blinking rapidly as if awaking from a dream, he heard the applause and shouts and saw the smiling faces below.

He bowed three times and ran off again, not stopping until he was safely on the other side of the caravan, in the dark. A moment later Clarence and Esmeralda were congratulating him, hugging him and telling him how well he had done.

"I'm so proud of you," Esmeralda said, surprising him with a hug. "You were so totally wonderful. I couldn't take my eyes off you."

"Fantastic, Dex," Clarence said. "You really pulled it off. That was three times better than any rehearsal. The audience really pushed you to your best. That's what happens to a real performer. Tomorrow I'll give you some notes, just little things that might be improved. But really, you don't need me anymore. You're way beyond anything I know."

And then Frederick came up to him. He put out his hand and Sullivan shook it. "Good show," Frederick said, and walked away.

What Sullivan felt at that moment would have been impossible for him to describe. A great tingling excitement through his whole body. Tremendous relief that it was over. Pride and amazement. Happiness at his friends' affection for him. And, perhaps most amazing of all, a desire — no, a *need* — to do it again.

✳ 24 ✳

IT was during the dessert course at the Stardust Home for Old People that Elsa Fargo collapsed, sending her bowl of tapioca flying across the room.

It is a simple fact that in a house full of old people there is going to be a regular need for doctors, nurses, and ambulances. While Loretta, who had taken an advanced first-aid course, rushed to Elsa's side, Gilbert was already phoning 911. Within minutes the paramedics were carrying their equipment into the dining room as the other residents looked on.

Elsa's sister, Rita, stayed by her side. The younger sister (she was only seventy-eight) held Elsa's hand while the paramedics carefully put their patient on the stretcher. "You've got to be all right," Rita said, still holding her hand. "You just have to, Elsa."

"Oh, I'll be fine," Elsa said weakly. "I'm not dying yet. Not until Sullivan comes home. You hear that, Loretta? Gilbert?"

"We hear you," Loretta said, wiping away a tear.

After the ambulance was gone, the rest of the residents shuffled back to their rooms. Nobody watched television or played cards. When the telephone rang, Gilbert answered. It was a nurse at the hospital, saying that Elsa was all right and could come home tomorrow. Gilbert went straight to Rita's room to tell her the good news.

It was another hour before Gilbert and Loretta could retire to their own apartment. Loretta opened up the account books and began to sort through a pile of bills. Gilbert picked up his knitting but just held it in his lap.

"More than two months," Gilbert said. "It's been more than two months since Sullivan disappeared."

"And Jinny and Manny have been gone for weeks," Loretta said.

"It's unbearable," said Gilbert.

"Yes."

"And now we're getting all these calls from other parents whose children have gone missing, because of the classified ad. And so far, not one of them fits the pattern," Gilbert went on.

"So many missing children. And each of their parents still hoping to find them."

"Do you—do you think he's alive, Loretta?"

His wife paused. "I don't know. I suppose there's a difference between what I believe and what I *want* to believe. I know that I want to believe he's all right."

"And if he is alive, what do you think Sullivan's doing? Right now, I mean."

"I don't know. Missing us, I suppose. I only hope he's not too lonely or too miserable. I hope there's something good for him out there."

They lapsed into silence. It was late and they were tired and ought to have gone to bed. But neither of them moved.

❄

That night, Norval didn't sleep much. Mostly, he stared up at the ceiling and thought about Sullivan. He had this strange feeling that he and Samuel and Sullivan were in this together, like the Three Musketeers. Or the Three Stooges, maybe. Which made no sense, because Sullivan was gone. And how strange and pathetic, he thought, that it had taken Sullivan's death for him and Samuel Patinsky to become friends. If only Sullivan were around, just think what fun the three of them could have together. And how happy Sullivan would be. Instead of being picked on, he'd have another friend.

"I wish you were here, Sullivan," Norval said into the darkness.

Finally, he fell asleep. But at the sound of the alarm clock he jumped out of bed, tripped while trying to put on his pants, and tried so hard to pretend that everything was normal at breakfast that both his parents asked him if something was wrong.

He walked to school feeling as if some other personality had taken over his body. As he approached the front doors he saw Samuel waiting for him on the top step.

"Jeez," Samuel said. "You look like you're about to puke."

"I think I *am* about to puke. I've never done anything like this before."

"*Nobody* has ever done anything like this before."

"I mean, I've never gotten into trouble."

"Well, you're going to get into trouble now. Bigtime. You prepared for that?"

Samuel looked hard at Norval. Norval felt drops of sweat break out on his forehead, but he said, "Yes. I'm ready."

"All right then. We meet in the caf at lunch."

"Got it."

All Norval could do that morning was watch the clock. For him, the school day had always passed quickly, but today it crept along like a melting glacier. At last, the lunch bell rang. He went to his locker, pulled out his backpack, and headed for the cafeteria. The cafeteria doubled as an auditorium and there was a stage at one end. It was already crowded with kids lining the tables, and at first he couldn't see Samuel. But there he was, standing in front of the stage.

"Let's do it," Samuel said.

Norval looked over his shoulder to check for teachers and then pulled himself up onto the stage. Luckily, he had been a member of the crew for the most recent school musical, *Beans, Beans, Beans!* He slipped behind one of the curtains and used a rope to lower one of the flies that were used to hold up scenery. Once it was on the ground, he opened his backpack and unrolled the banner.

Norval and Samuel had made the banner together. Three bed sheets stitched end to end, it was an impressive six feet high and twenty-four feet long. Attached to its top at two-foot intervals were ties made from shoelaces, and now Norval used them to attach the banner to the fly, scrambling on his knees across the stage. Panting from both exertion and fear, he looked around for Samuel.

He was there, all right. Holding the principal's microphone in his hand. He gave Norval a thumbs-up.

"Here goes," Norval said, feeling as if he was about to seal his own fate. He went to the other side of the stage, counted to three, and then, as quickly as he could, hauled up the fly.

The banner unfolded perfectly. Next, he opened the curtains. Immediately, students began to notice it —how could they not, it was so large. They whispered, giggled, pointed. The red letters were enormous.

The unofficial, against-the-rules, fantastic SULLIVAN MINTZ CELEBRATION DAY!!!

"*Yes, ladies and gentlemen,*" Samuel shouted into the microphone as he strode to the front of the stage.

Everyone turned to look at him, and somebody called out, "Way to go, Patinsky!"

Samuel waved. "That's right. Today we're going to

celebrate the life of Beanfield student Sullivan Mintz. And we're going to start it off . . . by *dancing!* Do it, Norval!"

Norval had almost forgotten the next step! He tripped across the stage to the sound console. Samuel had already plugged in his MP3 player; all Norval had to do was press play. He turned the volume all the way up, hit the button, and the cafeteria shook with the beat of drums and the wail of electric guitars. When he turned, he saw Samuel actually starting to dance. Right on stage, by himself, rocking his big body, shaking his butt, pointing his index fingers out at the other students, all with an enormous grin on his face. Norval couldn't help laughing out loud. The lunchroom aides were laughing, too. *Man,* he thought, *if only Sullivan could see this.* More unbelievably, some of the students — girls, mostly — started swaying to the music. Then *they* started dancing! And then a few boys joined in!

"Yeah, baby, get down!" Samuel growled into the microphone. "Now, who's got a memory of Sullivan they want to share? I mean, he was a student here, right? He went to class with us, walked the halls. Some of you must have something to say. Don't be shy."

At that moment, Norval saw something that made

him freeze. Principal Washburb was moving up the aisle. Norval could see that he was shouting, but it was impossible to hear him over the music.

Washburb was having trouble getting through the dancing crowd. Somebody even elbowed him in the nose, knocking his glasses sideways. Turning again, Norval saw a girl pull herself up onto the stage. He recognized her; she was in the grade below them and always wore her hair in a ponytail. The girl took the microphone.

"At the beginning of the year," she said, "my dog died. He was old, but it was still really sad. I was crying at my locker and this boy came up and asked me if I was okay. I showed him a photograph and he said that it must have been a really great dog. He was just sweet to me, that's all. He made me feel better. I never even knew his name until I saw his picture in the paper. It was Sullivan Mintz. He was really nice. I guess I just want to say, 'Thanks, Sullivan, wherever you are.'"

The girl's eyes were shining. Quickly she gave the microphone back to Samuel and jumped down into the dancing crowd. "Yes, he was!" Samuel shouted, taking back the microphone. "Sullivan Mintz was a nice guy and we'll never forget him!"

"Sullivan Mintz forever!" somebody shouted.

"Sullivan Mintz forever!" the crowd shouted back.

Everyone danced.

Principal Washburb finally reached the stage. He hauled himself up, caught his breath, and marched over to Samuel.

"You and your buddy are in for a world of pain," he bellowed.

Samuel just kept on dancing.

* 25 *

LETTING GO

$\mathcal{S}$ULLIVAN performed the following night and
the one after that. Each time he grew a little more
confident, of his juggling and his acting ability both.
He started to sense more clearly the response from the
audience—anticipation, fear, amazement. He could
even tell when their attention lagged once or twice,
although he hadn't yet figured out how to tighten up
those moments.

Everything seemed different to Sullivan now. He
wasn't just a bystander, somebody watching from the

wings while the others performed. Now he, too, was a part of the show. When he was helping to set up the stage, he was also setting it up for himself. When he was going to sleep in the caravan, he was as tired from his performance as Esmeralda, Frederick, and Clarence were from theirs. When Master Melville sat down for dinner and said, "Eat up, my dears. You'll need your strength," he was talking to Sullivan, too.

And in small, subtle ways, the others treated him differently as well. Coming off the stage, Frederick didn't insult him anymore. Instead he would say things like, "It's an easy audience tonight," or "Watch out for the heckler in the second row." Esmeralda always noticed and complimented him when he did something particularly well. And Clarence, who had been his director, now talked to him like a fellow performer. Sullivan couldn't help marveling at all the changes.

After his fourth performance, as he gathered up props, Sullivan noticed that the line to buy bottles of Hop-Hop Drops was longer than usual. Could it possibly have anything to do with his act? As he stood watching, he noticed some people in the line looking at him and whispering, as if he were some sort of celebrity. He felt himself blush with pride and turned away to help Frederick bring down the stage.

When the camp had been cleaned up and the last

bottle sold, the other kids brushed their teeth in the field with cups of water. But Sullivan didn't join in or follow them into the caravan. Instead, he remained standing outside, feeling the cool air and watching Master and Mistress count the money and lock it in the metal box. He wasn't sure why he was waiting there. Perhaps he wanted Master Melville to say something more, to tell him again what a hit he had become. But no, it wasn't that. He realized it was Mistress he really wanted to hear from.

Mistress Melville alone had not once complimented his performance. When he came off the stage, he couldn't help looking to see if she had been watching him. But she was always tuning her banjo-ukulele or wiping down her harmonica. He didn't know why it should be important to him, when she was clearly a mean and cold-hearted person. Maybe it was that she was so pale and beautiful that a single kind word from her would mean more than a hundred from someone else.

Master Melville packed up the table and chair while Mistress picked up the money box. Perhaps now was the time he might coax her to say something. Even if all she said was that he wasn't terrible, he thought he would be satisfied.

She began to walk by. Quickly he said in an unnaturally high voice, "It was a good show, wasn't it, Mistress?"

She stopped. And looked at him. "Why are you talking to me, boy?"

"No reason. I was just —"

"And why are you standing there when you should be in the caravan? You're not planning to run again, are you?"

"No, Mistress, I wasn't. I only thought —"

"You thought? Why do you believe that you have a right to think anything? *I'll* be the one to tell you what to think. You had better understand that you are now a part of this medicine show. So get yourself ready for bed. You have to perform again tomorrow. And the night after that and the night after that. This is your life now, boy."

She walked away, the money jingling in the box. Master Melville put out the last lantern, and suddenly, it was dark. Sullivan heard low voices in the caravan, the snorting of the horse, a cricket starting to chirp in the tall grass. Master Melville came up and said quietly, "You must be tired. Time for a much-deserved sleep. Go on with you now." So Sullivan went on. He found his toothbrush and walked to the edge of the field, where he brushed his teeth. He went behind a tree to pee. He washed his hands and face in the basin that had been left out, then he tossed away the dirty water and clipped the basin to its place underneath the caravan.

He went to the back of the caravan and climbed inside. And then, as Master Melville closed the door and the room went black, and he heard the key in the lock, Sullivan remembered something. He remembered his parents, Gilbert and Loretta. He remembered his sister, Jinny. And Manny, too. He thought of Norval, his one school friend, and even, for some reason, of Samuel Patinsky. And he realized that he had not thought of them all day, not once. He had thought only of his performance on stage. Had looked forward to it, had hoped to succeed more than he had hoped for anything before, and when he had succeeded he gloried in the applause and shouts and praise. In all of that, he had forgotten the people back home. He had forgotten the family that loved him. And forgetting, even for that short time, felt like letting go. It had been a relief, he realized now, not to be missing them all the time.

The caravan began to move. Somebody turned over. Somebody else sighed in his sleep. Sullivan stared